ALEX WAGNER

Arsenic and French Lace

Penny Küfer investigates

1

"My daughter would never have taken her own life," Lucinda Schümann said—for what must have been the tenth time. Penny had given up counting. She felt sorry for the woman who had been her new client for exactly twenty-five minutes. But would she be able to help her?

Lucinda's mascara was runny, and her perfectly manicured fingernails were clawing at the handkerchief she kept dabbing her eyes with. She sniffled, sought Penny's gaze again, and continued, "Niní was so passionate, so talented, so full of life—she would never have committed suicide. I just know that. And certainly not with that nasty poison!"

"So, you think your daughter was murdered?" asked Penny.

Lucinda's eyes widened. "What? Oh my God—"

"That would be the only other possible conclusion, wouldn't it?" said Penny cautiously. "If Niní did not drink the poison herself, it must have been administered to her."

Lucinda swallowed but then nodded. "Murder," she whispered, "in my house. God help me!"

The police had thoroughly investigated this alternative; Penny already knew that much. And yet, in the end, the officers had confirmed the conclusion that had been there from the beginning: Niní Delight, twenty-six years old, daughter of Lucinda Schümann and head of a luxury lingerie chain, had poisoned herself. She had locked herself in her bedroom and swallowed a dose of arsenic that could have killed an elephant. And this, of all things, while her sister, Valerie Delight, famous burlesque diva, was performing her signature act just a few rooms away, lolling scantily clad in a champagne glass on stage.

Penny shook her head involuntarily, as if that could help her wake up from this bizarre dream. Only yesterday she had been bored and had hoped for a new case. No, already half desperately longed for it! And now she was sitting here, in the winter garden of Lucinda Schümann's luxury villa in Hietzing, one of the most fashionable neighborhoods of Vienna, between hibiscus bushes and small lemon trees, and was hesitating to take on this new case.

The only reason for her reluctance: it was probably *not* a murder case but rather the tragic suicide of a young woman—with the mother not being able to get over this stroke of fate.

Lucinda Schümann couldn't be blamed. How terrible it must be to lose one's daughter in this way, after she'd barely reached adulthood!

It had been neither Penny Küfer's wish nor her merit that she'd already stumbled into two murder cases before she had even completed her training as a professional detective. And into a third one shortly thereafter.

In the process, however, she had discovered one thing about herself: she had a passion for murder! That sounded macabre, of course, and she would never have said it out loud, but it was the truth, nonetheless.

For this reason, she had made a decision in early July: she wouldn't go on searching for a job in a detective agency, as the classic career path for professional sleuths would have dictated. Now that she'd had a 'taste of murder', spying on unfaithful husbands or pursuing thieving employees simply no longer appealed to her. The limits imposed by the law on private detectives were simply too narrow for Penny's newfound passion. For this reason, she had decided to go into business for herself. Not as a professional detective but as an amateur sleuth or a *very* private investigator. Neither, of course, was a viable job title that could be used in public.

For her last two murder cases she'd received fees so considerable that she'd be able to live on them for a few decades, assuming a halfway reasonable lifestyle. The people she'd helped with her sleuthing had been extremely generous.

Thanks to this nice financial cushion, Penny could dare to turn her dream into reality. She decided to pick up where a few lucky coincidences—or fate?—had brought her. *Murder* was the magic word. She would solve only capital crimes. She'd take on cases where, for some reason, the police had been unsuccessful. Cases where the officers got it wrong or didn't even get involved.

She was not allowed to call herself a professional or private detective in Austria. To do so, she would first have had to complete the necessary years of practice in an established detective agency. And professional sleuths were not authorized to solve murder cases on their own.

How about: *Expert in Suspicious Homicides*?

No, you could hardly have something like that printed on a business card. She needed something more inconspicuous.

After endless days of brooding, she had finally put the following sign on the door of the pretty little office she had decorated with much heart and soul:

Penny Küfer
Security Consultant

The same wording was on her brand-new website, that had cost her quite a bit of money, and also on the business cards she had printed.

She was ready for her first client! Alas, just after the start of this promising new career, not the tiniest murder case wanted to present itself. Not even a concerned grandmother worried about the safety of her pet cats!

The weeks passed, the beginning of July became the end of July, but her cell phone didn't ring once. And her brand-new e-mail inbox didn't receive a single inquiry.

But then, in the first week of August, she did receive a call. *Frederike Küfer,* it said on her cell's display.

An awful lot could be deduced about Penny's relationship with this woman by the fact that she was simply listed by her name in Penny's directory. Under normal circumstances, something else should have been written there: *Mom.*

Frederike, as was her way, didn't beat around the bush.

"A friend needs your help, Penelope. Her name is Lucy—that is, Lucinda. Schümann. I don't know if you've ever met her?"

"My help?" Penny asked incredulously.

She could hear Frederike Küfer taking a deep breath on the other end of the line. "Well, your services in the...profession you were so eager to take up. As a detective." The way her mother pronounced the words *profession* and *detective* made them sound like the worst kind of disease.

When Penny had announced last year that she wanted to start training at the detective academy, her mother had disinherited her on the spot.

Frederike Küfer was rich, arrogant, a master of financially rewarding marriages—and she wanted her daughter to follow in her footsteps. She had never made a secret of this. For Frederike, a career as a professional detective ranked somewhere between vermin exterminator and assistant cleaner in a penal colony.

And now this woman, of all people, was recommending a client to her daughter? Penny couldn't believe her ears. Her pride would have commanded her to simply cut off the conversation, but her curiosity and zeal got the upper hand. She finally had a case!

"Lucinda Schümann's daughter has recently passed away," Frederike informed her. "Just imagine the shame! A suicide in the family. Which wasn't one, though, if Lucy has her way."

"And I'm supposed to prove that?" Penny concluded.

"That's right. You reckon yourself capable to do that, Penelope?"

Penny hated it when her mother spoke in such a stilted way, even more so in a tone that made one think of a permanently stuffy nose. Which was not the case. Frederike Küfer's airways were just fine.

This way, Penny had ended up sitting right here, in Lucinda Schümann's winter garden. Niní Delight's suicide, which was supposedly not a suicide, had happened two weeks ago. The funeral—a cremation—had already taken place.

"Niní loved life, and she still had so much ahead of her," Lucinda was repeating in a tear-stained voice.

"Niní Delight...what an unusual name," Penny said, while still debating with herself whether she should take on this murder case, which probably wasn't one. She was well aware that Frederike Küfer wouldn't take no for an answer. And Mrs. Schümann didn't seem like she'd give up so easily either.

"Oh, Niní Delight—that was her artist name, of course," Lucinda said with a wistful smile. "My older daughter started using it first...Valerie Delight. She came up with that name because she needed something fanciful. A stage name for her burlesque art. But then she went all in on that pseudonym. And she has infected us all with it. Me and Niní. I find myself calling the girls by their new names, even when it's just us."

"So Niní was the younger sister?" asked Penny.

Lucinda nodded. "My sweet little bundle of joy! The most adorable baby you could ever imagine. And Valerie has always been her great role model. Niní adored her. Even as a child, she always wanted the same dolls, the same clothes like her. And Valerie's friends were hers, too."

Lucinda sniffled. But this time she blinked and pressed the crumpled handkerchief firmly into the corners of her eyes—probably to fight down another flood of tears.

"Ferdinand, my late husband, was...well, pretty conservative. He selected the given names for our girls. *Sophia* and *Charlotte*. Beautiful names, no question, but they never really fit the two of them. For burlesque art, of course, a stage name is needed. Something exotic, you know? And Niní followed suit. She was always my playful little kitten, full of crazy dreams and with boundless imagination."

And so now the sweet little kitten was dead. Penny had to admit that the image of Niní Delight, which had arisen in her mind's eye thanks to Lucinda's descriptions, actually seemed rather incompatible with suicide. At the same time, however, she knew that precisely those people who outwardly always appeared cheerful and seemed to be bursting with energy were sometimes afflicted by the worst depressions, and might, in the end, no longer see any meaning in their lives.

"Will you help me?" Lucinda asked in a pleading tone. "Oh please, Penelope, you must help me! I promise you: should you come to the conclusion that it was indeed suicide, I will close the matter. Make my peace with Niní's death, if it was indeed her act. Dear Frederike spoke so highly of you. She said you can bring even the most hopeless cases to a successful conclusion."

Penny was at a loss for words. Could it really be true that Frederike Küfer, of all people, had praised her detective skills in such a way?

But she had no time to dwell on this thought. Lucinda was already talking again—and she seemed to have heard a 'yes' when Penny had certainly remained silent. The mother, who had just been in tears, now sounded hopeful and all at once filled with ardent zeal.

"Can you get started right away, Penelope? Put your other cases on hold? I'll gladly pay you double your usual fee. And I'll set you up with a—how do you call it?—an operations center here in the house. My most beautiful guest room is all yours! I want you to work on this case day and night. I want you to understand how Niní lived, to get to know her environment...and us, her family. We are all at your disposal. My daughter Valerie, myself, and of course the staff."

Penny raised both hands to stop Lucinda's rant. It would be damn hard to admit failure to this client; that much she knew already. But turning down the case was out of the question as well. Not just because Frederike Küfer wouldn't take no for an answer. There *was* something strange about this case, and Penny's detective instincts had been aroused.

She steered the conversation back to a detail that Mrs. Schümann had mentioned when describing Niní's death. It had seemed odd to her, and she wanted to know more about it. "You said earlier that Niní had been talking about 'a day to remember' on the eve of her death."

Lucinda nodded vigorously. "That's what she said. *Tomorrow is my big day, Mom. Love at last!* Those were her exact words. And then, when they found her, all dead and lifeless, she had laid out a charming new dress—and a corset she had sewn herself. A masterpiece, I tell you! These things were just waiting to be worn and admired. And then Niní is supposed to have taken her own life? Tell me honestly: does it make any sense to you?"

"Not really. But that doesn't mean—"

That was as far as Penny got. Lucinda had risen from her fauteuil and hurried over to a bureau that stood beside one of the wrought-iron columns of the winter garden. She returned with a silver frame containing two portrait photographs and pressed it into Penny's hands. "Look at them! My two girls. My princesses."

Penny could tell her new client was fighting tears again. She took the photo frame and looked at the two young women. It had to be a relatively recent picture. Niní clearly looked a bit younger than Valerie, but both were of the age Lucinda had mentioned. Mid-twenties, only a few years younger than Penny herself.

Both Valerie and Niní were as flawlessly pretty as Disney princesses. Penny, who was generally quite satisfied with her appearance, suddenly felt rather plain. She was often asked about her beautiful, natural red hair, and she certainly attracted the occasional glance in other ways, too— not that she cared very much about that. But next to Lucinda's daughters, she felt like the proverbial ugly duckling who would never turn into a beautiful swan.

Valerie's mane of hair fell over her shoulders in jet black and perfectly styled curls. She was the dark, mysterious type. Niní, on the other hand, wore her hair shorter and in platinum blonde. Her eyes seemed huge—just an artifact of the photograph? She was smiling at the viewer full of trusting innocence, reminiscent of a newborn fawn. Lucinda had really described her deceased daughter accurately. She looked full of life. Exuberant. Full of energy and drive.

And now she was dead. Because she herself had wanted it that way? Or because someone else had felt a deadly hatred for this doe-eyed beauty?

2

Penny raised her head and looked into Lucinda's expectant eyes. If Mrs. Schümann had not given birth to her daughters when she herself had been a teenager, she had to be at least in her mid-forties now. She didn't look a day over thirty-five, though, and was just as attractive as her girls. Good genes, you might call it.

"You'll just have to help me," Lucinda repeated. "You will, won't you?"

Penny hesitated no longer. "All right," she said, "I'll do my best." *For you—and for Frederike,* she added in her mind.

Lucinda thanked her half a dozen times, then Penny managed to ask another question that was on her mind.

"Mrs. Schümann, you mentioned earlier that Niní's, uh, death day was also Valerie's big day. Your older daughter announced her engagement, didn't she? To—what was his name?"

"Alex Adamas. You'll get to meet him. The best son-in-law a mother could ask for!"

"Then isn't it possible Niní was talking about her sister when she mentioned the big day thing? Valerie's great day, not her own?"

Lucinda shook her head. "Oh, she was talking about *her* big day, I'm sure of it. We didn't know then that it was going to be one for Valerie, too. Val didn't tell us a word about her upcoming engagement. She only invited us to a very special party. That's what she called it. At our house. We have a very beautiful ballroom, still original from 1895. Wonderful Art Nouveau ornaments and frescoes, you really have to see it. That's where Val's party was held."

Penny promised to look around the house extensively, and Lucinda acknowledged it with a satisfied smile. Even though the wistfulness was far from gone from her expression. "I didn't think anything of it when Valerie invited me to the party," she explained to Penny. "She likes to do that once in a while. Usually when she's working on a new show and wants to test it out on her friends first. But on that day, after a few new acts, she gave her signature performance in the champagne glass—and that's when Alex proposed. It was sooo romantic, you can't even imagine!"

"And right after the show had ended—" Penny began.

Lucinda frowned. She nodded somberly. "Right after the show, we realized that Niní hadn't been there. We went looking for her, trying to find her in her room—"

Lucinda's voice failed her. "I'm sorry," she croaked, "I really need to pull myself together. Whining like a teenager won't bring Niní back to life."

She dabbed at the corners of her eyes again with the already crumpled handkerchief—smudging her mascara even further. "What I wanted to say: we looked for Niní but found her door locked. Locked from the inside. At first we were just standing around, puzzled, but then we broke the lock...and found Niní's body. It was horrible!"

Penny gave her a moment to collect herself, then asked, "Who was the man Niní was talking about? *Love at last—*

there must have been some guy involved, surely? Did your daughter have a new boyfriend?"

"Yes, I think there was someone," Lucinda said. "But that's where Valerie—or Alex, for that matter—will be more helpful to you. Niní very rarely spoke to me about her affairs of the heart. And when she did, she usually gave vague hints only. We live under the same roof, but I do my best to give the girls their privacy. They have long since grown up, and the house is fortunately large enough for each of them to have her own personal space. Her own life."

Lucinda looked around her winter garden as if to consciously appreciate the benefits of her home. Then she continued, "Niní has never had a longer relationship, though, I think. Nothing really serious. She often seemed to be in love, but just as frequently she was suffering from heartbreak. I could always sense that."

"So you don't know the guy's name...this new love interest of Niní's?" asked Penny.

Lucinda shook her head. "As I said, you'll have to ask Valerie. I'm sure she will know. I've only seen him around the house once or twice. A handsome fellow, and he seemed very devoted to Niní...but I don't think they'd been together long. At least, that was my impression."

"And that day," Penny continued, "had he been invited to Valerie's party, too? Was he in the house when Niní—"

She hesitated for just a tiny moment. If she was going to investigate a murder, she had to talk about Niní's passing. More than once. There was no way to spare Lucinda by beating around the bush.

17

"When Niní died," she said, striving to give her voice a sympathetic yet firm tone.

"I don't know if he was at the party," Lucinda said. "I don't remember seeing him. But there were a lot of guests there—and I knew only a few of them. Friends of Valerie and Alex's, for the most part. Or admirers of Valerie's art. She has many devotees, as I'm sure you can imagine."

"Forgive my ignorance, Lucinda," Penny said, "but I'm afraid I don't have a very precise idea of burlesque art..."

"You don't have to apologize for that," Lucinda said. "Most people these days can't imagine anything about it. Some just think it's a form of classy striptease. But it's so much more! An almost forgotten performance art. Valerie is the only truly professional burlesque dancer here in Austria."

Mrs. Schümann gave Penny a scrutinizing glance but didn't seem satisfied with what she saw in her face. Presumably Penny was still looking a little perplexed.

"It's about celebrating beauty and femininity," Lucinda continued. "Burlesque is a world of dreams, of beautiful appearances, of spectacle. The burlesque dancer hints at secrets that are never fully revealed. She weaves magic into our otherwise terribly sober modern world. She makes the withered imagination of the viewer blossom anew. Think of the film divas of times long past. They had style, embodied elegance, and they mastered the art of seduction without being vulgar. Valerie is following the tradition of these screen goddesses. She wears the most gorgeous dresses and lingerie, feather shawls, sequins...and classic make-up. She performs wonderful dance routines, presenting her body scantily clad, and at the end of her acts she might be wearing even less...that's true. Plus, of course she does bring very erotic scenes to the stage. But nothing ever looks cheap or even vulgar. You should definitely see one of Valerie's shows. Or attend a rehearsal—she usually does them at our house. Valerie practically works around the clock. She's a perfectionist and never satisfied with herself."

"So that means Valerie does this...full-time? Can you put it that way?" asked Penny.

"Yes. She earns her own living. And not a meager one, I think. Although, financially, Niní was certainly the far more successful of the two. Valerie is an artist, so it's not so much about profits. But both girls are self-employed; have been for years. Ferdinand, my late husband...he was a pharmacist, you know. He left enough money for my living expenses and for the upkeep of the house, to which we are all very much attached—and a little beyond that, a modest annuity for the girls. But the two of them have been very go-getting and ambitious from the start, and they are both partial to luxury. As am I myself, I'm afraid."

She smiled, as if to beg forgiveness for this bad habit. "The girls earn their own money, and they are proud of it."

Penny nodded. She was just looking for the right words to praise Lucinda for her well-bred daughters, as the situation called for—when a young man appeared among the tropical plants of the winter garden. He stepped out from behind one of the lemon trees as if he had magically materialized there.

He had dark hair, was slim and tall, and perhaps in his early thirties, Penny guessed. A faint smile was playing around his lips. It died, however, when he noticed Penny.

"Oh, you have a visitor, Lucy," he said. "I'll come back later then, I didn't want to interrupt—"

He turned to leave, but Lucinda held him back. "Nonsense, you're not interrupting. On the contrary, you're just in time, Alex. I wanted to introduce you two to each other anyway. This is Penny Küfer, a detective I've just hired. Her mother is an old friend of mine. Penny, this is Alexander Adamas, Valerie's fiancé. I'm sure you know his jewelry stores, don't you? Alex is incredibly capable. He didn't inherit anything but built his entire business himself. And at such a young age."

There was unmistakable pride in Lucinda's voice—she was probably as taken with her prospective son-in-law as she was with her own daughters. "Alex is currently staying in our house," she added, "Well, more or less. He's been an important support to Valerie during this difficult time." She gave the young man a sympathetic look.

For a few seconds Alex seemed confused, but then he took a step towards Penny, who had jumped up from her armchair. He held out his hand to her and gave her a warm smile that emanated from his eyes. They were gray-green, those eyes, and for a moment it seemed to Penny that she was losing herself in them.

In an instant, however, she regained her composure. "Pleased to meet you," she said with a bit more formality than she had intended.

"A detective?" he asked.

Penny had the impression that this fact didn't exactly delight him. Or was she just imagining it?

3

"Why don't you join us, Alex?" Lucinda urged her would-be son-in-law. "I'd be grateful if you could assist Penny a bit. Would you please take care of everything she might need? Answer her questions...whatever is necessary."

Penny's first impression had not deceived her. Alex Adamas did not seem to share Lucinda's enthusiasm for the employment of a private investigator in the least. The friendly smile was still playing around the corners of his mouth, but at the same time he seemed reserved, perhaps even hostile.

Penny couldn't help but take a closer look at Valerie's fiancé. He was in no way inferior in terms of attractiveness to the burlesque dancer who would soon become his wife.

However, while Valerie looked like a perfectly styled art figure, Alex's good looks were of the all-natural and completely laid-back variety. He radiated a kind of charismatic aura that immediately made you feel at ease. He was wearing a simple black T-shirt and dark blue jeans—both very unobtrusive garments. On his left hand, however, Penny spotted a striking man's ring with a deep blue gemstone that immediately caught her eye.

Back to business, she admonished herself—but Alex took the floor before she could say anything. "You've hired a detective, Lucy?" he repeated his earlier question. "Because of...Niní?"

"Security consultant, to be exact," Penny cut in, but Lucinda brushed that quibble aside with an impatient wave of her hand. "I want the truth, Alex," she said.

Her tone was now no longer tearful but very determined. "The truth!" she repeated emphatically. "No matter what it looks like. But until then, I will not accept that Niní should have taken her own life. Since the police won't listen to me, I've just taken matters into my own hands. And Penny will prove that I'm right!"

Penny wanted to object. "I can't promise that—" she began, but that was as far as she got.

Lucinda was in full swing now, and it was obvious she was a very assertive woman when she wasn't overcome with grief. "Penny needs an operations center at our house. The guest room on the second floor. The corner suite. Will you let the maid know, Alex? And take care of everything Penny might need, will you? She must not want for anything. She's kindly agreed to get started right away and give priority to our case."

Penny had done nothing of the sort, but she didn't think it wise to bring it to Lucinda's attention. In truth, she had no other case to put on the back burner, but she certainly wouldn't say so out loud.

Alex gave Penny a furtive look that could only mean one thing: *Lucinda is just deluding herself. She doesn't want to accept her daughter's suicide.*

Penny did not return the gaze. She could not allow herself to agree with that assessment, not even silently. Even if she had very similar thoughts of her own. Now that she had accepted the case, she would do her best to support Lucinda's theory. And to find Niní's murderer—if he actually existed. Mrs. Schümann was her client now, and Penny owed her full commitment, no matter what the result of her investigation would be in the end.

Lucinda rose with the grace of a young dancer.

"Alex is all yours," she said to Penny. "In the meantime, if you'll excuse me, I need to lie down for a bit. I want so much to be strong for my little Niní, but I'm afraid all this is taking more out of me than I care to admit. I've got a nasty headache."

She added a few quick words of farewell, then she was gone. Penny and Alex were left alone and looked at each other for a moment, perplexed.

Then the young jeweler took the floor. "Well, if you please—I'll show you your *operations center*." He spoke in a dramatic tone, indicating a gallant bow, the corners of his mouth twitching treacherously. He seemed to have a hard time suppressing a laugh. But at least that was better than his reticence just a moment before.

"Well then...let's go," Penny said. *What have you gotten yourself into again?* she asked herself.

Alex guided her through the spacious house like a knowledgeable tour guide. Almost every detail of the villa seemed to be original from the nineteenth century. And both the architect and the interior designer had probably been outstanding representatives of Art Nouveau. Penny admired the mosaic tiles, the stucco elements, the ornate railings of the marble staircase that led up to the second floor, and especially the pervasive colored glass elements, both in the windows and on the chandeliers that illuminated the staircase and hallways.

This villa was the perfect home for colorful birds of paradise. Very fitting for Lucinda Schümann and her daughters. Now, however, an oppressive, almost eerie silence lay over the house, as if the old building were a sentient being mourning the loss of its vivacious young occupant.

Alex Adamas led Penny into a sumptuous room filled with antiques, old oil paintings, and precious textiles. Wall hangings, carpets, curtains, even the wallpaper were shimmering silkily. A few dust motes were dancing in the golden sunlight falling through the large windows. A balcony door stood open. A flowery breeze was wafting in from outside, a few birds were squabbling loudly, and the villa's garden was in full bloom. Actually, it looked more like a park than merely a garden. Penny counted dozens of treetops, and wherever she looked, manicured paths of white marble gravel meandered between the trunks. She also spotted countless ornate statues and finally an ivy-covered arbor that looked very inviting from up here.

As Penny tore herself away from the sight of the beautiful garden, she noticed that Alex was eyeing her expectantly with his gray-green eyes. The smile they constantly seemed to be radiating had now become even friendlier.

"What do you want to start with?" he asked. "And how can I help you?"

He was really damn handsome, this fiancé of Valerie. But that was probably to be expected.

Penny tried to focus on the task ahead of her. *Prove that Niní did not take her own life.*

She hadn't put it so explicitly to the grieving mother, but one thing seemed clear: if Niní had indeed been murdered, the perpetrator was probably part of her immediate circle. Poisoning someone was a very personal matter.

Penny asked Alex to tell her about Niní's death again—from his point of view. However, she learned hardly anything new. The police had ruled out foul play because Niní had locked her door from the inside. The only thing found in the room was a small glass vial that had contained the arsenic. Just Niní's fingerprints were on it. So she must have ingested the poison voluntarily; no wonder the police had come to this conclusion.

All the other people in the house at the time of her death had been at Valerie's party. In the ballroom. In full view of everyone else. Same with the staff. The entire three-person team—consisting of cook, butler, and maid—was busy feeding the crowd of thirty or so guests. No one had had the opportunity to murder Niní.

"And certainly no motive!" Alex added emphatically.

"Niní's environment...can you give me an overview?" Penny continued, unperturbed. "Who were her closest friends?"

Alex didn't have to ponder for long. He began to enumerate: "Her best friend was, of course, Valerie. The two of them adored each other. But she also got along famously with Saskia. Saskia is...*was* Niní's right-hand in the company. A very successful lingerie chain, but Lucinda must already have told you that."

Penny nodded.

"Niní also got along well with Tony, who is often here at the house. Valerie's manager, her coach...quite priceless, the man." Alex fell silent, seeming to be pondering something.

"Go ahead," Penny encouraged him. She had dug a slim notebook out of her purse and was writing down everything Alex told her.

He shrugged. "I don't know anyone else, I'm afraid. Niní was married to her work or rather to her art. Her lingerie was commercially successful as well, but that wasn't what she was about. She loved to design, to sew, to shop for fabrics... She was always planning, brainstorming, prototyping—or whatever you call it with lingerie. I'm no expert on that," he said with a disarming smile. "Niní attended fashion shows, visited hip competitor stores, and any event that inspired her in any way. She was always on the go. I'm sure she had other friends I didn't know about. Valerie will be able to tell you more about them."

"You're a jeweler, Lucinda mentioned?" asked Penny, a little out of context.

There was something about Alex that wasn't exactly conducive to her concentration. When he looked at her the way he was doing just now, it threw her off. On the one hand, there was something like professional respect in his gaze—as if he considered her a great expert in the field of criminology. But there was something else in his eyes, too. Something Penny couldn't interpret, and that irritated her.

"That's right," he said. "I'm a jeweler. Although I'm no longer running the retail stores myself. I only manage a few special key accounts now. And I deal in gemstones—that's my greatest passion." There was a flash in his eyes, as if to emphasize his words.

"What about Niní's boyfriend?" Penny went on. "Do you know him?"

Alex nodded. "You mean Lars? I don't know if they were truly a couple. He's come to see her a few times over the last weeks. I don't live in the house myself, after all, at least not officially—though I guess I'm spending most nights here at the moment." He furrowed his brow and blinked mischievously at Penny. As if he had something to apologize for.

"Lars, then..." she said, "and his last name?"

"Lars Simon. I think he and Niní had known each other for a few months at most."

"And what was their relationship like? Did you happen to overhear any arguments or something of the like?"

Alex shook his head. "I think they got along fine. He seemed to be quite in love..."

"And Niní?"

Alex hesitated for a moment. Then he shrugged. "It's hard to say. But Valerie might know more."

"What does he do for a living, this Lars Simon? And do you have his address or phone number?"

"Sorry, no idea."

"Well, I'll ask Valerie about it," Penny said.

"Yes, do that. If you want, come over tomorrow night. Actually, you're going to be staying here now anyway, aren't you?" he corrected himself. "Valerie's working on her new show, rehearsing several nights a week. Here in the house. That's where you can meet the people I told you about earlier. Saskia Prinz—Niní's right-hand woman. She's taken over from Niní when it comes to dressing Valerie. Plus Tony. Tony Varga."

"Valerie's manager and coach, you said?"

"Exactly. I myself will also be at the show rehearsal, sort of as an audience. There will be a small dinner where you can talk to everyone, interrogate them or whatever you have in mind. And of course you can also get to know Valerie. She's been rehearsing with a lot of zeal these days, it seems to me. Almost doggedly sometimes. She really wants to do the new show, despite her loss. She hasn't postponed our wedding date either. Niní would have wanted her to not give up—and to be happy with me. These thoughts keep Val going," he added.

Was Penny imagining it, or did Alex's expression darken a bit at those last words?

Don't jump to conclusions, she admonished herself—as she so often did when taking the first tentative steps in a murder case.

The thought made her smile. *So often...*as if she were already a super-experienced sleuth.

In truth, she was still at the very beginning. And she had no intention of letting her initial success go to her head. Every murder case was different, and the risk of failure was high. She was not fooling herself in that regard.

"Did any of the people you've mentioned to me hold a grudge against Niní?" she turned back to Alex. "Was there a dispute in the last few weeks? Or any prior incidents I should know about?"

Alex shook his head wordlessly.

"Can you think of any other reason why someone would want to murder Niní? "

"No! That's just it. I really think she committed suicide. As horrible as that might sound. I'm sorry."

"It's okay."

For a moment, the two were standing in silence in the middle of the luxurious guest room—Penny's new operations center, if Lucinda had her way. Penny watched the golden dust motes dance and couldn't help but spontaneously think of gold and diamonds. Which was undoubtedly because of Alex's profession. Jeweler and gem dealer. That sounded exciting.

Penny was not like her mother; she was not addicted to luxury, pomp and riches. But she liked precious stones. And pearls, too. Little miracles of nature.

She pushed the thought aside and turned to Alex once more. "What about you?" she asked. "How was your relationship with Niní? Did you get along well, you and your prospective sister-in-law?"

"Yeah, sure."

The answer came too fast. Much too fast.

Penny waited for a moment, but Alex didn't want to add anything. So she followed up with another question, "For how long have you been dating Valerie?"

"Six months, more or less."

Pretty short time to be engaged already, Penny thought.

"If something feels right, I'm not one to hesitate," Alex said, as if he had read her mind.

4

It was early evening by the time Penny returned to her apartment.

Lucinda Schümann would certainly have insisted that she spend the night in her new 'operations center' as early as tonight—but with her client down with a headache and only Alex Adamas to represent her, Penny had had no trouble excusing herself. "I'll need to pack some things and get some equipment from my office," she'd explained, and Alex had raised no objections.

After amassing a nice nest egg thanks to her last few cases, she had realized a dream and moved to the first district, Vienna's old town, full of winding alleys, magnificent palaces, but also warped, old houses.

The residential building in which her new apartment and adjoining bureau were located belonged to the latter category. The building was over three hundred years old, had a steep gable roof, tiny windows with rickety shutters, and in the courtyard ivy grew over the facade and the wrought-iron balconies. The house stood in a small alley that was closed to car traffic. Only the occasional Fiaker, the old-fashioned horse-drawn type of carriage popular with tourists, rolled over the cobblestones here.

Penny's new apartment was situated right under the roof. On the third floor of the house was her bureau, which consisted of two rooms, and above that lay another two where she had set up her private living space. To get up there, one had to climb a spiral staircase so narrow and steep that it felt like climbing a church tower.

Now, however, Penny headed for her bureau. It consisted of a reception room for clients, with a conference table and some comfy armchairs. Behind that was her office or rather her library. The showpiece of this second room was an antique fireplace—no longer usable but giving the room a wonderfully historic feel.

She hadn't been able to resist a little homage to Sherlock Holmes, the master detective: with the help of a switchblade knife, she had pinned a bundle of old letters to the wooden mantelpiece. A bit of eccentricity must be allowed in her profession, she thought.

The room's only window boasted a view of St. Stephen's Cathedral. Well, you had to bend your head quite a bit to see it. But still. And on the other walls of her office, she had already amassed a book collection to be quite proud of. Lots of reference tomes on everything from criminology to forensics. Plus psychology, interrogation techniques and a nice little collection on murder methods, including poisons. She now pulled one of these volumes from the shelf, wanting to learn more about arsenic. After all, this poison played the key role in her new murder case.

Penny turned the pages and her mind started spinning. If Niní had indeed been murdered, how had the perpetrator managed to so convincingly fake a suicide? How and when had he administered the arsenic to her? Had the poison vial found in her room just been a ruse? Skillfully planted by the murderer after he'd got Niní's fingerprints on that thing at some earlier time?

The hypothetical killer must have been at the villa that day and at least for a short time near Niní. He would hardly have put some poisoned food or drink in a random place, in the hope of Niní ingesting some of it.

Penny focused on the entry about arsenic in the poison encyclopedia she was flipping through.

Arsenic is the poison of kings—and the king of poisons, the introduction read.

Very aptly put. The history of this diabolical substance was quite fascinating. Cleopatra already had known the deadly power of arsenic, it was said. When the legendary Egyptian queen decided to end her own life, she had initially considered this poison. In the end, however, she decided against it—death by arsenic was too painful, and one did not make an attractive corpse when one passed away with the help of this substance. Well, Niní's hypothetical murderer had probably not been bothered with these concerns.

However, the question arose why Niní had not called for help when she had noticed the first signs of poisoning. Pain, nausea...why had she simply remained on her bed, behind her locked door? Wasn't that another—and a particularly convincing—indication of suicide? *Niní didn't call for help precisely because she wanted to die ...*

Penny continued to read. The famous Borgias in the Renaissance had been very adept at using arsenic. And Napoleon might have been eliminated with the help of this poison, as some conspiracy theories would have it. Even before the French Revolution, arsenic murders had been so widespread at the royal court that the poison had been given the nickname *poudre de succession*. Inheritance powder.

It was not until the 1830s that a British chemist first succeeded in detecting arsenic, and from that time on more and more poisoners ended up in court, or rather in the gallows.

But arsenic had also been abused in its long history as a kind of intoxicant—one that was even given to horses to boost their charisma and temperament. And among humans, too, there had been the notorious arsenic eaters.

In modern times, arsenic turned into a popular pesticide and was also successfully used in medicine. Of course, in far lower than lethal doses. Syphilis patients had been treated with it, and recently even arsenic compounds were being researched that could be effective against cancer.

Only a very small amount of the inheritance powder was needed to send an unloved person to the afterlife. The lethal dose already started at 0.1 grams. Moreover, arsenic was colorless and had neither a taste nor smell. The perfect murder weapon.

Death could be a few hours away if one took arsenic. However, it could also come much faster if one dosed more generously.

According to Lucinda's statement, Niní had taken a very high dose. How high exactly would probably prove impossible to find out. Penny couldn't just drop by the nearest police station and ask to see the case files. Being an independent sleuth had its drawbacks. Or rather, a security consultant.

But Niní must have been poisoned shortly before her tragic death if the dose had indeed been that high. Which in turn only allowed for a perpetrator who had been present in the house some time before the start of Valerie Delight's surprise party.

Penny went over the notes she had taken while talking to Alex Adamas. She skimmed the names he had given her. Saskia Prinz, Niní's right-hand woman in the lingerie empire. Tony Varga, Valerie's coach and manager, who also seemed good friends with Niní. Lars Simon. *Niní's great love?* Penny had written under his name. With a very big question mark. Was it because of him that Niní had hoped for a big day, as she had announced to her mother? Or was he the reason why she wanted to end her life? Penny had to find out, but this puzzle seemed solvable to her.

Alex Adamas had mentioned another name Penny had also written down in her notebook: Arthur Zauner, Lucinda Schümann's fiancé—since a short while.

"Arthur keeps calling Lucy his future wife," Alex had explained, "but we haven't heard anything about an official wedding date yet. I'm sure he loves Lucy, but—" At this point Alex had hesitated, and the usually striking twinkle in his eyes had given way to a somber look.

"I'm afraid I don't like Arthur," he elaborated when Penny inquired. "Valerie and Niní are sort of fallen girls to him. Erotic dance and sexy lingerie—harbingers of hell in his

36

eyes. He's a horrible prude, extremely misogynistic if you ask me, and bossy and moody to boot. Quite the patriarch living in the wrong century."

Scandal at Valerie's engagement party, Penny had noted down. Arthur Zauner had been invited to Valerie's surprise party along with Lucinda. The two of them accepted, of course, but Lucinda might have changed her mind if she had known what the surprise at this particular party would be. It wasn't the announcement of the engagement that led to the disaster, but the fact that Valerie performed one of her most popular show acts beforehand. Her lolling in an oversized, bubbling champagne glass. The burlesque diva was wearing blood-red, heart-shaped stickers on her nipples—and not much else. After the end of the act, Alex climbed onto the stage, got down on his knees in front of the glass and proposed to Valerie in front of the assembled guests. Valerie, of course, accepted happily.

Penny could still remember Alex's beaming smile when describing this special scene. For Lucinda's new partner, on the other hand, the idea of asking a semi-naked woman to get married, and in public at that, was probably the last preliminary stage to hell.

Unsuspecting as she was, Lucinda Schümann had thought the party in question a good time to introduce Arthur Zauner to her daughters. With a lot of people present, one could get to know each other while keeping a certain distance.

"Lucy had been seeing Arthur for several months," Alex explained, "but she had only brought him to the house two or three times up to that point, just briefly introducing him to her daughters. Now, of course, we know why. The guy is the worst kind of uptight moralist!"

The act in the champagne glass had barely ended when Arthur Zauner jumped up and stormed out of the house, ranting savagely.

"I think Lucy wanted to go after him at first," Alex said. "But then she came to her senses. Valerie was more important to her at that particular moment. But for the rest of the show, I saw Lucy crying silently and clutching her wine glass with trembling hands. She really didn't deserve that kind of treatment. No one does!"

Alex reflected for a moment, then added: "Maybe it was because of this terrible incident that no one missed Niní. We didn't even notice she wasn't in the room. I myself, of course, was completely focused on my proposal. I concentrated on not slipping up or tripping over my own feet when I climbed onto the stage. I was so nervous. And Lucy was probably thinking Niní might just be late—then she had to cope with Arthur's embarrassing outburst. When we finally realized Niní was missing after the show, it was too late."

"Which table would she have been at?" asked Penny.

"With Lucy and me," Alex replied. "We had our table at the very front, closest to the stage, for the family. Lucy, Arthur, yours truly...and Niní, whose seat just remained empty."

Lucinda Schümann had not mentioned a single word about Arthur during her conversation with Penny. Wasn't that strange? Was she ashamed of her fiancé because he'd behaved so outrageously?

At the end of his report, Alex mentioned that Arthur Zauner had been a permanent guest at the villa since Niní's death. He'd been sleeping there every night, not with Lucy of course, but in one of the guest rooms.

"It probably boils down to *no sex before marriage* between the two of them," Alex had said.

5

The suggestion Alex Adamas had made—that Penny should get to know Niní's immediate environment at Valerie's show rehearsal the next evening—turned out to be quite helpful. So did Lucinda's 'operations center' for Penny, even if this offer had sounded rather excessive at first. Staying in the villa and being a dinner guest or spectator at the rehearsal was an unobtrusive way to meet the most important people. Talking to a private eye scared people nowhere near as much as being interrogated by the police, but in the context of a cozy dinner chat, Niní's friends and relatives would certainly be even more approachable. At least, that's what Penny hoped.

So she made sure to arrive at the Schümann's villa shortly before the agreed time. She parked her car in the street, lined with old trees, leading to the house. Away from the thoroughfares, the district of Hietzing had still retained its almost village-like character of days long past. No building was higher than three stories, and spacious gardens and parks surrounded the individual houses and villas. Most of them were a good one hundred years old, judging by their architectural style. And there was nothing to be seen or heard of the busy car traffic of the modern city. It was an expensive neighborhood but also a beautiful one.

Penny herself had grown up just a few streets away but hadn't come here in a long time, due to the fall out with her mother.

She rang the bell next to the magnificent wrought-iron gate of Villa Schümann and was immediately let in. Under the likewise wrought-iron canopy in front of the main entrance, a young woman was waiting for her, dressed up like a Hollywood diva. However, not one that could have been attributed to the modern era. Although she was very young, her hair, makeup, cream-colored lace dress, and reptile leather heels looked like relics of the 1940s or 1950s.

"You must be Valerie," Penny said as the young diva put on a rather tense smile in greeting.

The woman nodded. "Penny, isn't it? Come on in."

"You in costume already for your rehearsal tonight?" Penny asked as the two climbed the marble stairs in the hall. A bit of polite conversation to break the ice—that's how the remark was intended.

"Costume?" Valerie repeated, peering down on her perfectly sculpted body.

Then she smiled in understanding. "Oh...no, this is my everyday outfit. Burlesque is a way of life for me, you know? Not something I put on or take off just for the duration of a show. I guess I was born in the wrong era, but I love glitz and glamour wherever I am. Even at home. I celebrate the female body, if you will. I never want to be less than perfectly dressed or made up. I wouldn't feel comfortable."

"I see," Penny muttered and squinted down at herself. She was wearing jeans that had seen better days and a rather bland sleeveless top. Her unruly, red hair was gathered into a ponytail at the nape of her neck. And as for makeup—did colored lip balm count?

Valerie must have spent a good half hour in front of the mirror for her makeup—Penny understood that much about this art. She herself would only ever apply some mascara or a bit of lipstick. And just on special occasions. Her mother had made every effort to turn her into a kind of doll like herself. But in the end, Frederike grudgingly had to admit to herself that she had failed with this plan.

You're not going to a beauty contest, Penny reminded herself, just as Alex Adamas was turning the corner at the top of the stairs. Which put the disconcerting and most outrageous thought into Penny's head that perhaps she should have dressed up a little prettier after all. *Celebrate the female body*, as Valerie had so cornily put it.

She found herself shaking her head. What was this nonsense about? Alex was the fiancé of a diva—and not to mention one of the suspects in her new murder case. She couldn't rule anyone out, no matter how irresistible his smile.

When Alex caught sight of his fiancée, it only enhanced his charismatic aura.

"There you are, sweetie," he said after greeting Penny with a quick nod. "Shall we get started? Everything's set up in the arbor, the food's ready, and Tony and Saskia are already here, too."

He reached out an arm and pulled Valerie to him. He looked at her as if he'd never seen a more perfect woman in his life. Tenderly, he kissed her on the temple while she closed her eyelids with pleasure.

Penny couldn't help it, she was overcome by such sudden sentimentality at this sight, it suddenly choked her throat. Alex seemed to really be in love with his fiancée. The way he talked to her, looking at her tenderly, was like a promise. *I will always be there for you.* And Valerie adored him just as blatantly—even though there was a hard, long-suffering expression in her eyes.

Alex was clearly the protector type—not the kind of man Penny usually longed for. She wasn't a helpless bunny who needed a strong hero by her side in order to cope with life.

Still, she couldn't fight a sudden feeling of terrible loneliness. She had not allowed herself this kind of sentimentality for months. Or rather, she had kept such emotions perfectly in check. She generally liked being single, coping with life without a guy. Even though she'd already been engaged once herself. It had not been meant to be...

Valerie gently extricated herself from her fiancé's arms and seemed to remember she had a guest. She walked a few steps ahead and then glanced over her shoulder at Penny while continuing to climb the stairs on her high heels. "So Lucy hired you? A female detective? That must be an awfully exciting job."

Penny nodded. Did it mean something, Valerie's referring to her own mother as *Lucy?* Just as Penny herself had entered her mother as *Frederike Küfer* into the contact list of her cell phone? Was this suggestive of family tensions, in Valerie's case, too? Or was it just another idiosyncrasy of a young artist who called herself Valerie Delight?

The young diva put on a winning smile. "We'll do everything we can to support you, Penny! Won't we, darling?" She gave another adoring look to her fiancé, who was walking beside her. "Maybe it will help Lucy cope better with Niní's death. If you can ever get over something like that. I'm missing my little sister like an arm and a leg. I don't know how I'd manage without Alex." Again, she shot him a tender look. Which Alex immediately returned.

Penny swallowed. The case was going to be tougher than expected, no matter what crimes she might ultimately uncover.

When they arrived outside the 'operations center', Penny's guest room, Valerie immediately turned to leave.

"Take your time settling in, unpacking and stuff, Penny," she said. "You'll find us in the garden later. If you take the gravel path to the left that branches off directly from the driveway, you'll get to our arbor. We're having dinner there. See you in a bit then?"

Valerie didn't wait for an answer. The room's heavy oak door slammed shut behind her and her fiancé.

Penny looked around her new stomping grounds. She hoisted her suitcase onto a low dresser, unpacked a few clothes, and stowed her pistol in the bottom drawer. In the homey atmosphere of the room, which smelled of polished wood and summer flowers, the gun seemed quite out of place. But you never knew.

She was generally not the type of person given to gloomy premonitions—but all of a sudden, she was overcome by just such a feeling. A creepy sense of foreboding. It seemed to her that something dark and threatening was emanating from the walls of this venerable old villa. Something that could become dangerous to her if she wasn't extremely careful.

What was wrong with her?

6

The sight of the garden arbor made Penny forget all dark premonitions in one fell swoop. This inviting clearing in the villa's park exuded the charm of an enchanted paradise. An almost full moon already hung in the sky as dusk was falling, and Penny made her way to the small group gathered for dinner in the arbor.

Evergreen hedges framed a massive teak table surrounded by softly upholstered garden chairs. A canopy overgrown with wild roses stretched above the seating area, the creamy white blossoms exuding a delicate fragrance.

Alex took it upon himself to introduce Penny to the two people present she didn't yet know.

Saskia Prinz, Niní's right hand in the lingerie chain, was small, wiry, and radiated a sober elegance that contrasted sharply with Valerie's playful, almost fairy-tale beauty. Saskia was wearing her dark blond hair in a tight ponytail and a woman's suit that must have been expensive. The cut and fabric had style but would have been a better fit for a law office than for a garden dinner followed by a burlesque rehearsal.

Tony Varga, on the other hand, looked just like it might be expected of an artist, according to the usual clichés. A nocturnal creative who detested regular working hours and only came to life at dusk. He was wearing dark sunglasses, which he didn't remove until the shadows between the trees swallowed the last light in the garden. Tony was dark-haired and possessed the slender but well-trained figure of a dancer.

Both he and Saskia seemed to already be in the know about Penny and what her presence in the house signified. She had hardly taken a seat at the table when the two of them started drilling her with questions.

Penny readily provided information about the daily work of a detective in general and about her assignment to investigate Niní's death in particular. If she managed to establish a certain personal connection with the two of them, she would certainly have an easier time later on when it was up to her to ask the questions.

Barely ten minutes had passed when Paula, the Schümanns's maid, served the first course of the dinner menu.

The questions stopped. People pounced on the appetizer as if everyone in the group had gone hungry for weeks. And when Penny tasted the first bite, she knew why.

"Emma, our cook, is a true genius," Valerie commented. "If you're not careful, you'll gain a few pounds in the next few days!"

Penny could only agree with her. The salmon pâté on asparagus tips would have done credit to a gourmet restaurant.

"Isn't your mother going to join us?" she turned to Valerie before bringing the next delicious bite to her mouth. "Shouldn't we be waiting for her?"

Valerie made a face. "Lucy's having dinner indoors. In the dining room. With Arthur, her fiancé. And before you ask why: because he hates us. Well, now it's just me. Since Niní—" She left the sentence unfinished. Instead, she placed one of her perfectly manicured hands on Alex's arm. As if that could provide her support.

"Arthur detests us," she continued with fervor. "He would never eat with us—with me—at the same table. He's calling us Lucinda's fallen daughters. And not just behind our backs. I guess I'm something like the Whore of Babylon to him. Female depravity in person. The ultimate blasphemy."

"I see," Penny said slowly. She mustn't take sides in this family drama she'd stumbled into.

Valerie's dark eyes were glowing with anger. "And Lucy does absolutely nothing, you know. She's certainly not a shy person, never at a loss for words...but with him? He can go on about me all he wants, she behaves like a purring kitten in his presence. And lets him get away with any impertinence. Any!"

After soup had been served, Penny managed to ask Valerie a few questions about her sister's death. "Is it true Niní didn't know the real purpose of that party you were throwing? I'm a little surprised you didn't tell her about your upcoming engagement when you were such good friends?"

Valerie smiled in anguish. Surely it wasn't easy for her to go over her sister's death again, even more so with a complete stranger. "I didn't tell her 'cause I didn't want *anyone* to know. It was supposed to be the perfect surprise. And Niní could be a terrible little chatterbox at times, babbling first and thinking afterwards. I didn't want her to misspeak in front of anyone and ruin the surprise."

Alex, sitting next to Valerie, was telling Tony about a recent visit to a gem fair in Hong Kong. Penny couldn't help but prick up her ears, although she really wanted to concentrate on her questioning.

Alex seemed to love his job very much. He was gesturing animatedly with his hands, laughing a lot and speaking in such enthusiastic words about rubies, sapphires and pearls as if they were living beings.

He has something of an adventurer about him, it went through Penny's mind. But at the same time, Alex seemed like an artist. And a scholar.

Only now did she realize that Valerie had probably asked her a question. The beautiful young woman was looking at her expectantly.

"Um, sorry, w-what did you say?" Penny stuttered. How embarrassing. Fortunately, Valerie didn't seem incensed that it was her fiancé, of all people, who had provided this distraction.

"I asked you if you were implying that one of our guests— at the party—murdered Niní? You said she must have been administered the poison shortly before her death."

"It sure looks like it. But I'm not drawing any conclusions yet," Penny tried to dodge the question. A part of her mind was still drawn to Alex's description of his trip. Now he was talking about precious stones called *spinels*. And he was claiming they were able to rival the coveted rubies in brilliance and beauty.

Damn it, Penny, focus!

She quickly turned back to Valerie. "I'm gathering the facts first," she explained to her, "only then will I start putting the pieces of the puzzle together, building theories and testing them."

"Almost sounds like a scientist," Valerie said.

"Well, I wouldn't describe it in such lofty terms; it's just detective work." She quickly changed the subject, coming to the next point she wanted to clear up with Valerie. "Niní's friend, this Lars Simon, do you know him well?"

Valerie shook her head, her dark curls bobbing, draping around her shoulders in new waves. "Not at all," she said. "I don't think Niní was serious about him. She could get any man she wanted."

"Any idea how I could get in touch with him? Would you have a phone number, or do you know where he works?"

"No, sorry." There was regret in Valerie's perfectly made-up dark eyes. She glanced at her wristwatch; a tiny thing set with sparkling diamonds. "Now, would you excuse me? I need to set up a few things for the rehearsal. In the meantime, enjoy your dessert, and I'll see you later!"

Without waiting for a reply, she stood up, wrapped her arms around her fiancé's neck and placed a kiss on the top of his head. "See you in a minute, darling." Then she set out to follow the gravel path leading back to the house.

"Where will the rehearsal take place?" Penny turned to Alex.

"In the ballroom. But it's going to be a little while." He winked at Penny as if to say, *I speak from experience.*

Penny took the opportunity to turn to Tony before Alex could hog him again. Valerie's manager was sipping his orange juice. He hadn't touched wine or beer the entire dinner.

He was just plucking a dead flower from a hibiscus bush growing at the edge of the arbor. Just within Tony's reach. "I can't bear something dead—in the midst of all this beauty," he explained, his gaze not roaming over the flowers and trees but following the path where Valerie had just disappeared.

Penny gave him a sympathetic smile while mentally preparing her questions for him.

He, however, didn't give her a chance to speak up. He plucked off another completely shriveled flower and said, "They fired the gardener, you know. And he was a real artist." He sighed. "Death has taken up residence here ever since. Just look around!"

With a dramatic gesture of his hand, he pointed to the wild roses entwining the arbor. "I just hope Lucy will hire someone new soon. But, oh—" At last, he seemed to realize Penny probably didn't want to talk gardening with him.

"How can I help you?" he asked, looking rather dreamy and melancholic than determined to be of real help.

Penny started with some small talk, to warm up, so to speak. How long had Tony known Valerie and how had they met? What were his exact duties as her manager-slash-coach?

Tony smiled as he started reminiscing. "Oh, I've known Val for a long time. Originally I was planning a career of my own as a dancer... But you know how life goes. I was pretty talented, but nobody wanted to hire me. At least, no troupe that was any good. So, after a few years, I gave up dreaming of a stage career and opened my own dance studio instead. I started scouting and training young talents...and that's where I met Val. She was still a nobody, just an ambitious girl who was born fifty years too late and wanted to perform like the revue stars of yesteryear. Complete with the lascivious yet tasteful shedding of clothes." He grinned.

"And you became her teacher?" asked Penny.

"First, I became her lover." Tony acknowledged Penny's surprise with a wink. "Well, I'm hot, sweetie, I can tell you that! No, I can even prove it to you. Anytime, whenever you want." He put on a smile that was probably meant to be seductive.

Didn't he realize that it was Penny's job to investigate Niní's death? Was he really coping with this terrible loss quite as easily as he was pretending to? Or was his daredevil attitude just hiding the grief he had to be feeling?

"What was your relationship with Niní like?" Penny asked straightforwardly.

"What do you mean?" It came back promptly. "I was *her* lover once, too, if that's what you're alluding to. I'm sure you've been told that."

He eyed her briefly, his demeanor suddenly quite serious. "You haven't? Well, never mind. It was just a brief...what-

52

ever. Back when I was dating Valerie as well."

"You mean at the same time?"

"Well, first I was with Valerie. It was through her that I got to know Niní in the first place. And she was incredibly keen on me, you can't imagine! How could I say no?"

"And how did Valerie take that?" Penny asked.

"Oh, like I said, it was just a fling... First, they both wanted me, then suddenly none of them did. Hey, we were still kids, sort of. Valerie forgave her easily. I think it happened quite often back then, the two of them dating the same blokes. But it really didn't mean anything. The girls loved each other much more than any guy. They did everything together. Shared everything. Even their bed partners, back when we were young and wild." He smiled melancholically. You would have thought he was an old man musing about his lost youth.

His brow furrowed. He lowered his voice. "I miss Niní. She was so full of good vibes, a real bundle of energy. You should have met her! I'll never understand why she—"

He suddenly swallowed hard and averted his eyes.

"Why she committed suicide?" Penny asked cautiously. "Do you really think that's true?"

The corners of his mouth twitched contemptuously. "Well, what else? No matter how much we hate that idea. I know you're supposed to be snooping around here cause Lucy can't cope with things. And hey, I don't blame you. You got a living to make. I'm sure you get a lot of clients who just want to throw money out the window because they can't handle the truth. They cling to some crazy theory."

Penny didn't respond to that remark. "You come here, to the house, quite often, I suppose?" she asked instead.

"What? Yeah, sure. If it gets late and we party a bit, I'll spend the night here, too. There's plenty of room in the fancy mansion. And as I said: if you're also looking for a little fun tonight..." He lasciviously ran his tongue over his lips.

The guy was really impossible. Penny wasn't attracted to him one bit, even though Tony was undoubtedly handsome.

As if by magic, her eyes wandered over to Alex Adamas. To her astonishment, she noticed that he was looking at her—and had probably been listening carefully to her conversation with Tony. Whatever this might mean. It was probably nothing more than curiosity on his part.

7

"I should get going," Tony said, "Val's going to need me." With these words, he wasn't the only one to stand up. Alex probably took them as a prompt to head inside as well, where his fiancée would shortly begin her show rehearsal.

Only Saskia Prinz didn't seem to be in a hurry. Paula, the maid, had just brought her a second helping of chocolate cake.

Saskia briefly chatted with Paula, and both women praised the cook's baking skills in the most euphoric tones. From the brief dialogue that ensued, Penny could tell that Saskia liked to enjoy a second serving of dessert quite regularly. Where did the slim blonde put all those calories?

Penny hesitated for a moment.

Should she follow the guys, who were just disappearing behind the next hedge down the garden path? Of course, she wanted to see Valerie in action—but the chance to have a one-on-one conversation with Saskia seemed more valuable to her. She couldn't let something like that pass her by.

So she gently joined in the conversation between the two women and agreed with the praise of the cook. She didn't have to lie about it. The chef truly was a genius.

"Could I get a second piece of chocolate cake, too?" she asked the maid. That way she had a plausible reason to linger a bit longer in the arb and to have a first chat with

Saskia about Niní's death.

As an icebreaker, she asked Saskia a similar question like Tony before: how had she and Niní originally met?

Saskia's answer was less surprising than that of Valerie's coach. "Oh, I was one of Niní's first employees in her very first business. Wasn't five years ago. We've grown insanely since then." She smiled broadly, and the pride on her face was unmistakable.

"I'm good with numbers, you know," she continued. "And in sales. Niní was more of an artist. We also became friends in private, and we complemented each other perfectly, in Niní's eyes. She promoted me to manager and later her partner. And we were doing incredibly well. Niní started with a tiny store in a second-rate location, and now we have our flagship store on Kärntner Straße. It doesn't get any better than that in Vienna, does it? Plus, there are already more than ten other branches. Some of them abroad, in Munich, Paris, Milan. And we're continuing to grow."

The enthusiasm in Saskia's voice was unmistakable. Not only did she seem to be a capable manager, but she also seemed to put her heart and soul into her work.

"So, who's inheriting all this, now that Niní has passed?" Penny continued. Her money was on the beloved sister, but Saskia's answer took her by surprise. "I'm the sole heir," she said, with a touch of pride.

"Not Valerie?" Penny blurted out.

Saskia shook her head. She started to answer but then seemed to think better of it. She glanced around quickly, probably to make sure no one was within earshot. Then she said, in a conspiratorial whisper, "I think the truth is that they didn't love each other quite as much as everyone likes to think. I've heard them quarreling quite often."

That was interesting. Penny picked up on this thread. "Especially lately?" she asked, as casually as possible.

But Saskia wasn't dumb. She grasped immediately what Penny was getting at. "Hey, I didn't mean to say they hated each other to death and that's why Valerie served her little sister a poison cocktail! Of course, they were friends, but they were also having some pretty heated arguments from time to time. Ever since I've known them, anyway. Which doesn't have to mean anything. Niní was very temperamental—and so is Valerie. I just think that the two of them were putting up this one-heart-and-one-soul act mostly for business reasons. At least that was my impression. Valerie is a fantastic testimonial for Niní's lingerie—just the right brand ambassador for marketing. And Niní used to outfit her with the hottest pieces in return. All unique, hand-sewn items; something new for every show. And of course, the two were Mama Lucinda's little princesses. I think, also for her sake, they pretended to be closer friends than they really were. In truth, each of them had their own circle of friends. Or rather, Valerie had a circle of friends, and Niní threw herself into her work. She was a real workaholic. Although, of course, she still knew how to enjoy the finer things in life, if you know what I mean. Anyway, the two sisters didn't get together all that often. Just mostly for business, like I said."

"How did Valerie take it when she didn't inherit anything?" asked Penny. "Did she know about it before Niní died?"

"Yeah, sure. Niní already arranged it that way last year. She said I would carry on her business in her spirit if anything ever happened to her. She was very proud of her company; it was her baby, so to speak. And she probably wanted it to be in the most capable hands."

Saskia truly doesn't lack self-confidence, Penny thought.

"Besides, Valerie doesn't need an inheritance", Saskia continued. "She has enough money, just throws it around."

"Are burlesque shows that profitable then?" asked Penny.

"Nope, I don't think so. But the family is super rich. Just look at that house!"

"Yeah, huh," Penny said. Then she struck out in a new direction. "The day of Niní's death, were you at Valerie's party, too?"

Saskia's eyes narrowed a little. "Sure. We were all there. But before you ask, I was late. Arrived literally in the last minute before it started. So I didn't poison Niní, if that's what you're implying."

"Oh no," Penny said. "I'm not implying anything. I'm just gathering data. It's my job, don't hold it against me." She put on an innocent smile, and Saskia seemed to relax again.

A brief pause ensued, with both women dedicating themselves to their chocolate cake, then Penny went on, "You mentioned you were Niní's good friend in private, too. Not just her business partner. So what can you tell me about the mysterious man in her life? Niní spoke to her mother about a new love. That she had finally found her Mr. Right.

Who was he, do you know? Was she referring to this Lars Simon she was dating?"

Saskia pondered for a moment as she swallowed a bite of cake. "Hm, I don't think Lars was her great love. But there was indeed a man of her dreams. A guy she really had the hots for. Niní dropped a few hints but nothing concrete. She liked to be mysterious. Like in a soap opera. She had that much in common with her sister."

Saskia laughed but was wiping a tear from the corner of her eye the next moment. "Damn, I miss her! She turned my life into a theater play. Into a wonderfully colorful, crazy mess... But I loved it."

"Do you think it possible she committed suicide because of this guy?" asked Penny cautiously. "That she was in love with this unknown dream man, but he just didn't want her?"

Saskia looked at her in amazement. "Well, I wouldn't go that far. Drama—yes, Niní loved that. But suicide just because of a guy? Nope, I can't imagine that. Niní swore to me that this time it was the great, true love...but it wasn't the first time she claimed it. She liked to play with men. She never had a long relationship."

Saskia speared another piece of cake with her fork. Before she brought it to her mouth, however, she paused.

She tilted her head and looked at Penny. "Hmm, maybe it was different this time, after all. More serious than usual. And the guy was apparently hard to conquer. Niní even consulted some kind of counselor about him once. The woman called herself a *heart whisperer*. Cool job title, huh?

Pretty corny!"

Penny nodded with a smile but pricked up her ears.

"Niní loved such esoteric stuff," Saskia continued. "Horoscopes, affirmations, spells, requests to the universe. I don't know. It's not for me."

"Do you remember the name of this counselor?" asked Penny. "Maybe she can tell us more about Niní's mysterious chosen one?"

Saskia frowned. "Nope, sorry. I don't think she ever mentioned the woman's real name... But if you want, you can take a look at Niní's computer. In the office. Maybe she has bookmarked the website of this heart whisperer. Or at least you might find it in her browsing history. I think Niní chatted with her quite often."

"Good idea," Penny said. "So where is Niní's office located? I assume it's yours now?"

"We've been sharing it for a while," Saskia said. "It's in our flagship store that I told you about earlier."

She put the dessert fork on the edge of her plate and reached for her purse, which hung over the back of the chair.

From an inside zippered pocket, she pulled out a business card featuring a model in a corset and lace stockings. Beneath it was Saskia's name, followed by the title *Managing Director*.

On the back was the logo of *Delight Dessous* and the flagship store's address on Kärntnerstraße.

"Come by tomorrow if you want," Saskia said. "I'll be in the office all day. Then you can also get an idea of the company Niní has built. You'll love it, I promise!"

"Thank you," Penny said. "I'll be glad to come."

Saskia nodded. "We really should go in now, though. To Valerie's rehearsal. She needs an audience!"

8

It had gotten late.

Valerie's rehearsal in the ballroom had taken Penny into a world unknown to her. A world full of ostrich feathers, silk stockings, tiny pieces of lingerie made of the finest lace...and lots of naked skin. Naturally, the kind of show Valerie was rehearsing was more interesting to a male audience, but Penny had watched spellbound, nonetheless.

The old ballroom of the house still exuded the atmosphere of a hundred years ago. Once upon a time, people probably gathered here for evenings of chamber music. And for the private theater performances so popular with the nobility—and the upper middle class.

Several round tables had been set up in front of a slightly raised stage. At the frontmost one, Penny had found a seat next to the other audience members. Alex, Tony, and Saskia.

Valerie had a never-ending selection of costumes on display, which she peeled out of with grace and tingling sensuality. She was not ashamed to walk around half-naked—even between the individual acts she scurried through the room unclothed, got rid of the lingerie that was no longer needed, and slipped into new pieces.

Niní had indeed been a master of her craft. Penny had never seen anything quite as beautiful in any lingerie boutique compared to the pieces Valerie was putting on—and off.

Tony had been helping Valerie undress and change, bombarding her with instructions. "A little slower here! More hip sway! Smile, dear, make it look easy! Playful!"

Alex had been more of a quiet bystander, but Penny could sense how much he admired Valerie. And desired her.

Saskia had taken it upon herself to provide Penny with background info on the individual show acts and the art of burlesque in general. But in the process, she didn't let anything on about her own feelings. Did she admire Valerie as well? Or were there tensions between the two women— not least perhaps because of Niní's inheritance?

Penny was confident she would figure it out once she knew them a little better. For the first day of her new case, she was satisfied.

After the rehearsal had ended, Penny decided to retire to her guest room. Would the night bring new insights? Probably not. She was dog-tired, and there was little point in sneaking around like a house ghost and spying. She would certainly not catch Niní's murderer that way. Apart from the fact that his existence hadn't even been proven yet.

She was just turning into the corridor that led to her room when a man approached her. He was perhaps fifty years old, bald, and had the typical figure of someone who spent his life behind a desk and liked to eat well and abundantly. His limbs looked lanky with no discernible muscles, and his stomach protruded quite a bit. Instead of a greeting, he blocked Penny's way and eyed her condescendingly.

Surprised by this behavior, Penny didn't know what to say.

The man, on the other hand, was not at a loss for words. "Arthur Zauner," he said curtly but did not extend his hand to Penny or wait for her to introduce herself in turn. "I suppose Lucinda told you who I am?"

Penny didn't have to think long. *Lucinda's lover,* she almost said. But the man probably wouldn't have welcomed that choice of words. He didn't look like someone who had a casual way with words—indeed, from everything Valerie and Alex had said about him, he was a full-blown philistine.

"Lucinda's fiancé," Penny said, then, in the politest tone of voice, putting on a friendly smile.

"That's right. And you're that...snoop, aren't you?" He couldn't have put it more snidely–but she brushed it off. Resolutely, she nodded and kept smiling.

"I'm glad I've run into you," he said, "I wanted to have a serious talk with you anyway."

Next thing Penny knew, he launched into a veritable litany that she could hardly follow. Or rather, didn't want to follow.

"...by no means cause a stir...consider our good reputation...will not under any circumstances allow my future wife or myself to be gossiped about or involved in a scandal...already bad enough, with these floozies as daughters!"

Penny couldn't believe her ears.

"Floozies?" she repeated.

Arthur Zauner made a snide hand gesture. "You know exactly what I mean. One is a stripper, the other sells sex stuff. Sold sex stuff," he corrected himself.

Oh, my goodness, Penny thought. Full-blown philistine was an understatement.

"In any case," Arthur Zauner continued, "I'd like you to leave as soon as possible. I have no idea what Lucinda was thinking in hiring you. And why I wasn't consulted in this matter," he added indignantly.

Penny took a deep breath. She forced herself to remain friendly. "Well," she said slowly. "I've been given a job to do—and I'm going to carry it out."

"Job? Pah. To find a murderer who doesn't even exist? The demise of Lucinda's daughter was clearly suicide. The bare facts speak for themselves."

"The facts?" Penny repeated. Maybe she could at least elicit some information from this obnoxious guy. Some details about Niní's death she didn't know about yet?

He smiled condescendingly. "I see you have basic skills in manipulative conversation. You really think I don't notice how you're trying to make me talk? But you're banging your head against a brick wall with me. I will not be manipulated. I am a lawyer, you must know."

"Ah, yes," Penny said dryly.

He raised an eyebrow. He was still towering in front of her, with his bloated belly, eyeing her like an annoying insect. He continued, "From this bumbling attempt to elicit information from me, I guess I must conclude that you are not even familiar with the results of the police investiga-

65

tion. Which doesn't surprise me. After all, you have no official status whatsoever, do you? You are nothing more than a woman who is too nosy, and then you call yourself a...security consultant?"

Awkwardly, he dug her hot-off-the-press business card out of a jacket pocket and read from it. He must have taken that card from Lucinda. Penny could imagine all too vividly how he was already patronizing his future wife. Unbelievable that Mrs. Schümann was putting up with this.

"I completed training as a professional detective," Penny said. And regretted it the next moment. Why did she allow this creep to give her a roasting? He was not her client. She wasn't accountable to him in any way.

"Oh, is that so?" he sneered. "And which detective agency do you work for? Why isn't that info on your card? And what makes you hide behind that ridiculous consultant title? Everybody and their mother claims to be a consultant these days."

Next thing, he seemed to realize something. His eyes narrowed, but suddenly he smiled. It was a crooked, sly smile, reminiscent of a hyena. Not that Penny wanted to do injustice to these poor animals.

"But of course!" Arthur Zauner sneered. "As a real professional detective, you wouldn't be allowed to investigate murder cases at all, or at least only to a very limited extent. In real life, you just can't go snooping around wildly and 'solve cases' like in those stupid mystery novels you women love to read. Just the impertinence of thinking you're smarter than the police!"

"Do you want to give me the bare facts about Nini's death, as you put it earlier, or not?" Penny replied. Her patience with this guy was rapidly coming to an end.

He shrugged. The hyena smile vanished. "Fine by me. If I do, maybe you're at least smart enough to realize that you're just wasting your time here. And Lucinda's money."

Penny said nothing, just looked at him expectantly.

"Well," he began, wrinkling his nose. "There was a very high dose of arsenic involved, taken just before her demise. Death must have been very rapid. No food, no drink, no glass was found in the room. Only the vial, you see. Should you now want to mention the trick so popular in TV thrillers—forget it. The vial was not put there *after* we'd broken down the door. I was present in person, and I immediately noticed the vial on the nightstand."

He probably interpreted Penny's silence as perplexity on her part, which only made him warm to his subject. "Could the poison have been put into the vial later while we were rushing out of the room to get help? No. None of us remained in the room, it is true—but the murderer could hardly have expected his victim to kindly keep a suitable vessel ready for him on her bedside table, into which he could drip his poison after her body had been discovered."

His eyes fixed on Penny. "Do you understand? She wasn't poisoned. There was also no one standing next to her, forcing her at gunpoint to drink the arsenic. Because how would that person have gotten out of the room afterwards? The key was inside the lock and—before you ask—it wasn't turned from the outside with the help of pliers or something similar. In short, not the slightest evidence indicating foul play. The police officers know their job!" *Unlike you,* his gaze seemed to say.

Penny wanted to reply, but Arthur Zauner wasn't done yet. "Besides, the girl was lying on the bed when we found her. She didn't try to get help. She *wanted* to die, get it into your head!"

The girl? Could this husband-to-be of Lucinda's not even speak her daughter's name? Because she was such a floozy, as he'd called her?

"You're very well informed," Penny said, in a tone that was full of innuendo. The *one to be best informed is usually the murderer,* was the silent accusation behind those words. She could be beastly, too, if this Zauner asked for it.

He, however, overheard this undertone. In any case, he didn't react to it.

"Lucinda told me," Penny began, "that Niní had been talking about her big day and that she had prepared a pretty new dress and some very special lingerie. Don't you find that behavior strange when, the next moment, you want to take your own life?"

"Pah, what does it mean. The girl got one of her hooker outfits out because she wanted to meet some guy. And he stood her up, I guess. I don't know."

"Didn't the police check Niní's last phone calls? Surely they could have reconstructed whether someone canceled an appointment with her?"

Arthur Zauner wrinkled his nose contemptuously. "I don't know anything about that. But why should the police bother with that when it was clear from the start she'd committed suicide? It's commendable, I think, if for once taxpayers' money isn't wasted."

"Where had *you* been, by the way, in the hours before Niní died?" Penny asked abruptly. She had been polite long enough now, she thought.

She enjoyed Arthur Zauner's stunned look. He had probably not expected such a direct accusation.

He hissed, "None of your damn business!" and with those words he turned around, leaving Penny standing there.

9

The next morning, Penny paid a visit to the flagship store of *Delight Dessous*. She not only wanted to get an impression of the company that Niní had built but also to deepen the conversation with Saskia Prinz—the heiress and new owner.

The store, located on one of the city's most expensive shopping boulevard, had huge glass fronts and exuded playful elegance, coupled with a touch of wicked eroticism.

Penny felt like she was entering the private salon of a Hollywood diva. Plush carpeting swallowed every sound of footsteps, a wide variety of lamps with colorful shades illuminated the room—just enough to allow for browsing of the exquisite range of nightwear, sexy lingerie, lace stockings and the like. The corners and the few open spaces of the store were bathed in shadows, suggesting endless nights of mystery and adventure to any lady who was willing to shop.

Penny spoke to one of the employees, who then disappeared into the back of the store to fetch Ms. Prinz.

Another lingerie consultant, as they were referred to on their little name tags, took it upon herself to show Penny around the store in the meantime.

"How do you like our new collection?" she chirped. "You're welcome to try something on, too. You'll feel like a goddess in this lingerie—and, of course, drive your boyfriend or husband out of his mind!" The saleswoman put on a broad smile and winked conspiratorially.

Why was Penny suddenly thinking about Alex Adamas' sparkling green eyes at those words? What was her subconscious trying to tell her? That these hot lingerie pieces were just the thing to seduce the fiancé of a burlesque diva?

What a ridiculous thought. That would never work. And anyway, she didn't want to seduce Alex Adamas at all—neither with lingerie, nor without!

Saskia Prinz brought Penny back to safe ground. She also gave her a tour—this time of the offices and warehouse. She was talking less about the various lingerie creations *Delight Dessous* had on offer and more about growth rates, profit margins, brand design and the like. She emphasized again and again that Niní's legacy was in the best hands with her. Was she ultimately plagued by a guilty conscience because she—as an outsider to the family—had inherited everything? While Valerie had come away empty-handed?

As they came to a halt behind the desk that had been Niní's, Penny said, "You mentioned this *heart whisperer* last night. The woman Niní turned to in order to win over her dream guy. Can we check on the computer and see if we can find this, uh, counselor's website?"

"Sure," said Saskia Prinz, dropping into the swivel chair and switching on the computer. In the browser which Niní had liked to use, she scrolled through the favorites bar and after a short time found what she was looking for.

"Ah, here it is. The Heart Whisperer—that was indeed the name."

She stood up and offered Penny her seat. "Feel free to check it out at your leisure."

Penny accepted the offer but only scrolled through the first few pages. She noted down the address of the website so that she could do some further surfing later on. But one thing was clear from the first glance: this consultant in love matters was not afraid to lay it on thick.

The pages were—both in terms of their appearance and their content—hard to top in terms of kitsch. Wherever you clicked, you inevitably came across pictures of couples in love, glittering little hearts, and euphoric reviews about the abilities of said heart whisperer.

"I owe her the love of my life," one reviewer had written. Another even called her a 'modern sorceress' whose rituals were the most effective they had ever tried. A third guy—yes, indeed a man!—praised an amulet he had bought from the heart whisperer, claiming that within a few days it had brought his now wife into his life.

Penny closed the browser and stood up. "And Niní actually believed in stuff like that?" she turned to Saskia. "Spells, rituals, amulets?"

Saskia nodded with a smile. "Niní swore by that woman. And believe it or not—one of the spells of this sorceress even led to a result! That wasn't so long ago."

Saskia pondered. "Maybe seven or eight days before Niní's...you know." She, too, still seemed to find it difficult to talk about Niní's death.

"What exactly did that spell do?" Penny asked.

"It led to Niní receiving a letter from her beloved. A card, to be precise. With one of those droll pictures on the front. The kind of thing that usually gets sent between people who are deeply in love. I can't remember exactly...heart-shaped balloons? Something like that. You know what I mean, right?"

Penny grinned. "I think so. And what did the mysterious stranger write? Niní didn't tell you who he was, you said yesterday?"

"That's right. Everything was top secret as far as this gentleman was concerned. And Niní didn't let me read the message on the card either. She just waved it under my nose and seemed intoxicated with happiness. She was really on cloud nine, I can tell you that much."

Niní's chosen one must have signed his message, Penny thought—at least she hoped so. If she could find the card, she might be able to solve the mystery of the man's identity.

Saskia had no idea what had happened to the card—but she and Penny agreed that Niní would certainly not have thrown away this token of love.

"Do you mind if I take a look around the office to search for it?" asked Penny. "Or have you already gone through everything and sorted out Niní's personal belongings?"

"What? No, I haven't gotten to that yet," Saskia said. "Feel free to look around."

No sooner said than done. Penny started with the desk

drawers, then rummaged through a half-height cabinet that stood directly behind it, and finally turned to the rest of the office's furniture.

In the end, she had opened every drawer, looked through every file folder, but hadn't found the slightest trace of the mysterious card.

"Does it matter that much?" asked Saskia. "Do you think the guy Niní loved, of all people, did something to her?"

Penny could have replied to her that, according to statistics, the vast majority of homicides were committed by lovers or spouses. But that seemed awfully cynical in this store full of playful lingerie that celebrated lust and love.

"It's just a possibility," she said simply. "We don't even know if it wasn't suicide, after all. But in any case, I want to find out who this irresistible stranger is, and why Niní made such a secret of him. I'm going to look around her room at home. Maybe the card is there."

Saskia nodded. "If you need anything else from me, feel free to come by anytime, okay?"

Penny thanked her and left the store – without shopping the latest collection of hot lingerie.

When Penny entered Niní's apartment at Villa Schümann, she felt like she was setting foot into the dreamy realm of a teenage girl. Niní had long passed twenty, but her private living space had not matured with her. The silk wallpaper was decorated with delicate flowers, the bookshelves were crowded with young adult novels—especially fantasy and romance—and the cream-colored furniture would have fit well in the nursery of an old country palace. Only a tiled stove in the middle of the living room was in Art Nouveau style, like the rest of the villa.

There was a floor-to-ceiling archway with a double door between the living room and the bedroom, and creative chaos reigned in both rooms. Not a speck of dust lay on the furniture, but on the shelves and in the drawers and cupboards Penny opened, there was mayhem. Everything was messy and cluttered. Finding a card here was like looking for the famous needle in a haystack. No matter though; Penny was determined to track the thing down.

She rummaged through lingerie and stockings in the drawers—where women liked to hide little secrets or valuables—but without success. In the drawer of the nightstand, she found birthday and Christmas cards from all kinds of friends but nothing that looked like a love message.

A thorough search of the cupboards and bookshelves took several hours, but in the end, Penny was rewarded. In a book that looked completely unread, she found the card Saskia had described. It was stuck in an envelope without a stamp, with nothing written on it except *For Niní*.

If Niní had used the card as a bookmark, the book should have shown signs of wear. At least a somewhat wrinkled spine. But this tome had not been read. The spine creaked softly as Penny opened the pages.

No, Niní had not carelessly used the card as a bookmark. She had deliberately hidden it in this book so that no one could find it. Which was only in keeping with her otherwise secretive nature when it came to the man she had apparently been very much in love with.

Was Niní afraid that someone from the house would snoop around in her room? The maid? Her mother? Her sister?

Something else gave Penny pause: there was no stamp on the envelope and no mailing address. Only Niní's first name. Which must mean that the mysterious sender of this card had delivered his love greeting personally. He could either have given the card to Niní himself or might have dropped it in the villa's letterbox. Or, option number three, had he slipped it under the door of Niní's room? Which would only have been feasible if he could enter and leave the Villa Schümann at will...

The front of the card actually had heart-shaped balloons on it, just like Saskia had remembered. Penny turned the card over and skimmed the text.

My dearest Niní,

I know how you feel.
Be patient with me, our time will come!

Yours,
A.

Be patient? Sounded like there was an obstacle that had to be overcome. And who was A.? That was the all-important question.

As many as three men who were regulars at Villa Schümann bore a first name that began with the letter A.

Alex Adamas, Valerie's fiancé.

But he had hardly been Niní's great love. No matter how good or bad the relationship between the two sisters might have been, Niní would certainly not have wanted to steal her sister's fiancé. She could have any guy.

Arthur Zauner, the mother's fiancé?

Not if Niní had possessed even the slightest bit of taste.

And finally there was Tony, Valerie's manager, whose real name was *Anton.* Someone had called him that a few times last night. Had it been Saskia? Anyway, he was the third candidate for the mysterious A. He himself had mentioned he'd once had a brief love affair with Niní. *A long time ago. Nothing serious.* That's how he had presented the relationship to Penny.

Could it be that Niní had suddenly been inflamed with new and exceedingly fierce passion for Anton-slash-Tony? That, too, was unlikely. And even if, why should it have been necessary to make a big secret out of it?

The man with whom Niní had been involved—at least superficially—in the last weeks of her life was named Lars Simon. Was there a nickname for Lars that began with A.?

Hmm, no, even that option seemed unsatisfactory to Penny.

There had to be a fifth man—one she had yet to find. Which she was determined to do. An outsider who didn't want to make the relationship with Niní public? Because he was married or something similar? But who had still asked Niní to be patient with him by sending her a card full of heart-shaped balloons?

10

The evening was already dawning when Penny finally left Niní's apartment. She had safely stowed the card from the mysterious A in her purse.

As she crossed the great hall to get some fresh air in the garden, her stomach spoke up. It gave a hungry growl that made her pause.

Penny glanced at her wristwatch. It was almost half past eight. She had probably missed dinner, but maybe the kind cook had a few appetizers left for her. She postponed getting some fresh air until later and made her way to the dining room. The cook's realm was right behind it—a fully equipped kitchen that would have served a small restaurant well.

Lights were on in the dining room, and when Penny entered the room, she found she wasn't the only late eater in the house. At the large round dining table in the center of the room sat Arthur Zauner, spooning up what looked like cream of vegetable soup.

Him of all people, it went through Penny's mind. Not exactly the dinner party one would wish for. But apparently everyone else had already eaten earlier. Not even Lucinda Schümann kept her sweetheart company.

Arthur raised his head and lowered his spoon. "You again?" he growled with undisguised hostility. "Are we snooping again?"

Fortunately, at that moment the cook entered the room. "Oh, Penny, it's you! You must be hungry! Make yourself comfortable, and I'll bring you something in a minute." A warm smile shone on her friendly face—what a contrast to the old curmudgeon at the dining table!

Emma didn't wait for an answer but hurried back into the kitchen.

Hesitantly, Penny took a seat at the table. Eating in the company of Arthur Zauner...how pleasant. But at least this way she had the opportunity to pester him with some more questions.

She didn't even bother to make polite conversation. Every friendly word was wasted on this guy. That was why she hit the ground running: "To get back to your alibi, Mr. Zauner—where had you been in the hours before Niní's death?"

The man jerked his head up and glared at Penny. Surely he wanted to say something, but she didn't let him get a word in. "Tell you what," she said, "I'm not going to let up until you're willing to make a statement. So let's just get this over with, shall we? I'm sure you don't have anything to hide. Or would you rather I complain to Lucinda that her fiancé, of all people, won't help solve the murder of her beloved daughter?"

Arthur Zauner deliberately brought a spoonful of soup to his mouth. Slowly and with control. Then, also in slow motion, he put the spoon down and reached for the napkin. He dabbed his lips with it.

Finally, he said, "You can look for the murderer until

doomsday—you won't find him. Because there is no murderer. Can't get that into your head?"

Penny dismissed the remark with a gruff wave of her hand. "So," she repeated calmly. "Where had you been on that day?"

He gave her an ice-cold stare, only to answer her question, after all, in the very next moment—much to Penny's surprise. It was clear from his tone how much she got on his nerves, but she didn't care.

"I spent the day in the library," he said, "here in the house. Lucinda has a wonderful collection of books."

"All day in the library?" Penny asked.

Arthur Zauner turned up his nose. "Surely you can't imagine that. Your generation doesn't know what to do in a place like that, does it? You only know cell phones, Facebook, endless TV series, computer games. But believe it or not, I spent the whole day in the library. And it was an extremely entertaining couple of hours. I read an excellent work on the crusades. Studying history is one of my hobbies."

"Did anyone see you during that time?" Penny asked.

"No. That is, Lucinda looked in on me once for a moment."

At that instant, the cook returned. She was balancing a steaming plate of soup on a silver tray, and Penny pounced on it immediately. As expected, it tasted delicious. Emma really was an artist.

Arthur Zauner used the resulting pause for renewed spitefulness: "Why do you actually do this job as a snoop?

You seem to come from a reasonably good family, don't you? And I guess you're intelligent enough that you could have taken up studies at university. At least in one of those fields you women like to choose. Communication studies or something similar. That would have allowed you to take up a respectable profession. Why become a snoop, of all things? That's almost as bad as my Lucinda's two nympho-maniacs!"

Penny put down the spoon. Which took her quite some effort because she would much rather use it to scratch out both of Arthur Zauner's eyes!

"My intelligence has been sufficient to get a degree," she said in a tone that betrayed nothing of her anger. Her voice was dismissive but seemingly completely composed. "If you want to be specific, even for a master's degree—with honors. Including some terms abroad at Oxford and at Harvard. Anything else you'd like to know about me?"

Her words had the desired effect. With his mouth slightly open, Arthur Zauner sat staring at Penny as if his own IQ had spontaneously halved.

Penny got up, carried her plate into the kitchen, and told Emma that the delicious soup had fully satisfied her hunger. Which was a lie. But better to eat out in a pub than have the most delicious dinner in the company of this sleazeball.

She returned to the dining room and crossed it with quick strides toward the door. She did not even glance at Arthur Zauner.

Only when she was halfway through the door did he seem

to regain his composure. In his peskiest tone of voice, he called after her, "Which university did you get your master's degree from, if I may ask? And what field of study?"

Penny did not deign to answer. She simply ignored him and let the door close noisily behind her back.

What an idiot!

11

Penny took a walk through the neighborhood, which was almost deserted at this time of day—first at a run to let off some steam. After that, she took a calmer pace and finally discovered a small sushi place a few alleys away, which looked very inviting. She went inside, found a romantic courtyard under giant old trees, and ordered a large portion of salmon sushi. Not quite Emma's cuisine but still very tasty.

Afterwards, she remained sitting at her table for a long time, leafing through her notebook and going over the facts she had gathered so far in her new case.

There was still no concrete evidence that Nini's death had been anything other than a tragic suicide. And realistically, Penny had no more than a few days left to come up with results. Arthur Zauner would certainly do his utmost do drive her out of the house as fast as possible.

Could he himself have had something to do with Nini's death in the end? He was a real monster—but a murderer?

When she returned to Villa Schümann a few hours later, shortly before midnight, the venerable old building with its columns, bay windows and golden Art Nouveau ornaments already seemed to be in a deep sleep. On the driveway leading up to the house, a few nostalgic lanterns flared up as

Penny was walking along, but the villa itself lay in complete darkness.

The night air was wonderfully warm and heavy with the scent of flowers. She decided to head to the kitchen for a nightcap and then make herself comfortable in the garden arbor for a while. Her brain was far from ready to stop working for the day, so sleep was out of the question anyway.

Not five minutes had passed after she'd settled down in the gazebo with a cup of hot chocolate when footsteps could be heard on one of the gravel paths. Then a rustling of grass. The next moment, a few twigs cracked to her left. There was something menacing about the sound that made Penny cringe.

"It's just me," a male voice said. "Alex."

Presently he was standing in front of her. As if he had just materialized—like a creature of the dark—into her world.

Penny had brought only a few candles for illumination, but Alex's green eyes seemed to sparkle even in that light.

"I hope I didn't scare you," he said. His voice had a warm, soothing tone.

"Uh, no. What are you doing here?"

What a stupid question. He lives here.

But Alex replied as a matter of course: "I saw light here in the garden. I thought maybe someone had forgotten to put out a candle. And we don't want to risk a fire, do we?"

He grinned then sat down next to her on the spur of the

moment.

"A beautiful evening," he said. "Valerie's already asleep, I'm afraid; she went to bed early. It hasn't been a good day for her. Headaches, grief for Niní...sometimes it goes quite well, but on other days I have the impression her grief is eating her up."

"I'm sure you'll be a great support to her during this difficult time," Penny said.

Alex hunched his shoulders. "I hope so."

Then his features relaxed again. "So how's your investigation going?" he asked with undisguised curiosity in his voice. "Any leads yet?"

Penny hesitated.

He looked at her expectantly but then seemed to realize. "Oh...I see. You don't want to talk to me about it? Top secret, your investigation?"

Penny pursed her lips. "I'm sorry. But that's just the way I work. It would be unprofessional to talk about the case with, um, involved parties. Sorry."

"Why not say *suspects*," Alex replied. He sounded hurt, but in the next moment he had already regained his composure. "That's all right. I understand. So you won't tell me anything. But *I* might have a lead for you! That's okay, I hope?" His smile returned.

Penny looked around. The few candles she had lit illuminated only the immediate area. The rest of the garden lay in complete darkness. But you'd certainly hear it when someone approached. They were alone and could talk undisturbed.

"It's almost a forest, isn't it?" Alex said. "Such a wonderful place. "

"Want to walk for a bit?" Penny heard herself say. "And you tell me what you've found out, okay?"

He agreed. As if on a secret command, they jumped to their feet at the same moment. Penny couldn't find her way in the dark, but Alex pointed her in the right direction. "This way. We can walk around the house and get back here at the end."

They trotted off. At first, Alex was striding along quite briskly, but then he adjusted his pace for Penny, who preferred to take things a bit more leisurely.

"I love this garden," Alex said after they had walked silently side by side for the first few minutes. "As for my own house...I live in Baden, you know. South of Vienna. And I don't have a particularly great garden. My property is tiny compared to this one. And I've never really cared about landscaping. Maybe I should hire a gardener sometime?"

He seemed to be talking to himself, as if he had completely forgotten Penny's presence. Polite chit-chat, nothing more. Was he feeling a bit awkward about this little walk in the dark?

The path they were following was quite narrow, so they had to move closer together if they were to walk side by side. Penny felt she could feel his body heat. And she could smell the tart notes of his aftershave.

He continued his little soliloquy, "I wasn't home much, always traveling the world before I met Valerie. Now I've canceled some trips to stay with her. And I've moved in here for the time being. Then, after we get married, we'll figure out where we want to live. If Arthur decides to move in with Lucinda, Valerie will want to leave anyway. On the other hand, she is very attached to her mother, especially now that her sister is dead."

He stopped abruptly. "But I didn't want to chat with you about gardens and houses and my wedding," he exclaimed, as if he had just remembered his real intent.

"I've tracked down Lars Simon! Nini's lost friend!" he added breathlessly, and in his eyes flashed something of the pride Penny knew quite well. Pride in one's own gumption because one had solved a tricky problem or found an important clue. The elation of having discovered an important lead in a difficult case. She loved that feeling—just like Alex seemed to do as well.

"I wanted to help you with your investigation," Alex continued. "And maybe I caught a bit of snooping fever myself. When you asked me about Lars, I realized that I really didn't know anything about him. So I did a bit of research. On the Internet. Of course, I'm an amateur, but I was surprised to find absolutely nothing about him."

Penny was about to respond, but Alex raised his hand. "Wait. Hear me out."

12

Penny looked at Alex expectantly, and he continued, "When I was about to give up on Lars, I remembered that he once gave me his phone number. Because he had watches to sell—and of course he thought that, as a jeweler, I might be able to help him with that. He used to be a collector of wristwatches at one point, he told me, but had now lost interest in them. He asked me about prices. I don't usually deal in used watches, but since he was a friend of Niní's, I promised him I would call a few contacts. Then...Niní died, and I completely forgot about it. And Lars never got back to me about the watches either."

They had come to a stop under a huge chestnut tree that cast such long shadows that Penny could barely see. It felt strange to be here alone in the dark with Alex on this wonderful summer night. There was something forbidden about it and exciting at the same time.

Focus on the case, she admonished herself. And asked, "You called him, this Lars?"

"I did," Alex said.

He started moving again, along the garden path. A few steps further, they triggered one of the motion detectors. The nearest lantern turned on. Penny could see that Alex was smiling—and looking a little dreamy. Was he enjoying playing detective and telling her about his adventures?

It sure looked like it. But at the same time, he was eyeing

her in a way that wasn't quite fitting. It was not the kind of look one would give a colleague with whom one shared an interest in a murder case, but the gaze of a man who took a liking to a woman.

Bollocks, Penny thought. *What kind of nonsense am I making up? It's probably just my imagination. Valerie—he's engaged to Valerie!*

Alex continued with his report, "I didn't want to jump right in with Lars about you, Penny. I mean about your getting involved 'cause Niní may not have committed suicide after all. I don't want any gossip around her death, it's not in the family's best interest."

"Yeah sure, no problem," Penny said quickly.

There it was again, that look, for sure!

No, he's just being friendly with you, that's all. And he has the kind of eyes that just keep smiling—that has nothing to do with you at all!

"I told Lars that I had solicited some offers for used watches. And asked him if we could meet sometime. I lied about the watches, of course, but the end justifies the means, doesn't it?"

"Sure," Penny said. She averted her gaze, forcing herself to look at the nocturnal garden. At the trees, flowering shrubs, the perfectly manicured flower beds. Anything but Alex Adamas.

"Lars was rather vague. He claimed he had a lot on his mind right now. He didn't seem ready for a meeting. Which struck me as odd because the other day he had been very eager to find a buyer for his watches."

"Hmm."

"And yet I got to meet him tonight! Thanks to a good bit of detective work—or so I think. You can be proud of me."

This time he smiled like a little boy who had solved a difficult task. And wanted to receive praise for it. This innocent smile made Alex's otherwise masculine face look even more attractive.

Damn it. Penny didn't understand why she had so little control over herself. This was a new experience. She wasn't the kind of woman who immediately lost her head just because she came face to face with a good-looking man.

"So how did you track him down?" she asked quickly. She finally had to force her rebellious brain to stay on task.

"When I called him and asked if he could talk for a minute, Lars said he was attending a performance at a summer theater. But they were in intermission, so he had a few minutes. When our conversation came to an end and he was about to hang up, I heard a woman's voice in the background. *Are you coming, sweetie?* she asked. That seemed suspicious to me. I mean, he was very fond of Niní. I had the impression that he was serious about her...and now, so soon after her death, he already has a new girlfriend with whom he happily goes to the theater? So I thought to myself: maybe he has known this other woman for a while—and he wanted to get rid of Niní because of her?! "

"But that would hardly be a motive for murder," Penny objected. "Nowadays, you just break up. You don't have to resort to such drastic means as murder."

"Yes, hmm...you're right about that, of course."

Alex seemed to ponder something for a moment.

Somewhere in the branches above their heads, a night bird was twittering away. It had gotten cooler, but now was not the time to run into the house and get a jacket.

Alex continued, "Anyway, from the few words Lars said back to this new girlfriend, I managed to deduce the play they were attending. Next, I found out where this play was being performed tonight—then I hopped in my car and got there without further ado. I arrived just in time, shortly after the end of the performance. And I spotted the two of them, saw them coming out of the theater, tightly embraced."

"Did you approach Lars?" asked Penny.

"Of course not! I followed those two. Secretly. They went out for dinner—to a cozy little place with its garden facing the street, where I could watch them. The woman seemed very much in love, and guess what, in the end she even paid for dinner. What a gentleman, that Lars!"

"And after that?" asked Penny, who was bursting with curiosity by now. There was something quite contagious about the way Alex was telling his story. He was making it sound like a great adventure.

"The two of them called a cab. And I—just like in a movie thriller—also got hold of one and followed them. They went to the nineteenth district, to a very posh address. A residential building with luxury apartments. But only she got out. Lars then rode on, to the fifteenth district—to a much more modest neighborhood. He got off at a block of flats on a street with heavy traffic."

"So they didn't spend the night together?"

"Nope—but I'm telling you, they're lovers! You should have seen them at dinner. The woman was devouring him with her glances rather than the food on her plate. I even videoed the two of them for you—with my cell phone."

He pulled the smartphone out of his pocket, swiped across the screen a few times. "I'm forwarding you the recording."

Penny nodded. "Good work, Watson," she teased. "With the video and her home address, I can find out who this woman is. And the exact nature of her relationship with Lars, too."

"Are you going to tail her?" Alex asked.

"I think I'll put a colleague on it. Something like this can get pretty intense in terms of required time, and I have other leads to follow. "

So now she *did* discuss the case with him. And she had to admit that she rather enjoyed having a kind of partner. Someone who lent a hand without being asked and with whom one could discuss the case. Especially in the moonlight in this wonderfully enchanted old garden. Which didn't change the fact that such an approach was highly unprofessional.

Penny was suddenly shivering, and Alex took off his jacket as a matter of course and put it around her shoulders. What was wrong with her that she suddenly had such a thick lump in her throat at this small gesture?

"You know what, I enjoyed it!" Alex said. He sounded surprised at his own words. "Of course, I'm a rank amateur, but this snooping, tailing, following...I liked it. It would be great if I could help you even more."

He looked at her questioningly but then went on talking when she didn't reply, "I think you're a very good detective, Penny. You're exactly in the right job."

He raised his hand so she couldn't protest. "I'm not saying this to flatter you. I was watching you, last night, conducting the interrogations. That is, they just didn't feel like interrogations at all, and that's why everyone talked to you so willingly. You come across as friendly, trustworthy and polite. A good listener who is a pleasure to confide in."

Penny couldn't help it—she had to smile. "I love my job," she said. "Every case is different, the stakes are always high, no boring routines..."

She could have told him how often she was completely in the dark. Or put her foot in her mouth. She could have confided in him about how Arthur Zauner had bawled her out. That this creep had made her look like the worst kind of amateur. And that she had almost lost her temper over it. But she refrained. She had to admit to herself that she really enjoyed the recognition Alex gave her.

He still sounded euphoric, "That's also what I like about my own job. No routine! Every day a new challenge. That's why I'm leaving my stores in the capable hands of my employees and have only picked out the most eccentric customers. I take care of them personally, even though sometimes I'd like to kill them when they're being super bitchy. And I love working on new, sometimes pretty daring designs for my jewelry collection. Which, of course, isn't half as exciting as chasing a murderer," he added with a twinkle in his eye. "So, as I said, I'd be happy to assist you again. I like being your Watson. Even though I'd much rather work with you on a case...a bit farther from home, if you know what I mean." He winced.

"There's something I wanted to ask you," Penny ventured forward. She had to confront him about this card Niní had received and see how he would react to the love greeting of the mysterious A.

She caught herself wishing it wouldn't bother him at all. That he had nothing to hide. She wanted to convince herself that he wasn't A.

Damn it, she scolded herself again. That kind of bias— she couldn't allow it. Not in a potential murder case. Alex was a suspect, just like everyone else!

She stopped, rummaged the envelope with the card out of her handbag and held it out to him. At first without further words.

They had just passed one of the lanterns again, so it was bright enough to read the card.

Alex also stopped and accepted the envelope. "What's this?" He pulled out the card and studied it closely.

"A?" he asked, frowning.

"Please tell me that's not your handwriting," Penny heard herself say. The next moment, she bit her lip. She really hadn't meant to put it that way!

A dark shadow flitted across the attractive features of her companion. With a stiff gesture, he handed her back the card and envelope.

"It's not my handwriting," he said brusquely. And right after that, "Let's go back to the house. It's getting late, and I have to get up early tomorrow."

What did that mean now? Was he acting suspiciously? Or was he just angry because she had accused him of having a fling—with his fiancée's sister, of all people? Was there a sudden sense of guilt in his gaze?

She couldn't tell. This man seemed to confound her intuition, which usually was quite reliable. And she couldn't deny that a part of her hated the fact that this wonderful nighttime walk had come to such an unpleasant end.

13

When Penny returned to her room, she felt she had been transported to the suite of a luxury hotel. Everything was spotlessly clean, the pillows on the bed were arranged like two swans, and her personal belongings, which she had carelessly dropped in random places, had been neatly arranged on the desk, on the bedside table, or sorted into drawers and cupboards. Everything was where it belonged.

The Schümanns' maid had done a great job. But most of all Penny was pleased with the pretty silver rimmed porcelain plate on the bedside table 'cause on top of it sat a huge piece of cake. It was lemon yellow with a golden-brown icing and smelled heavenly. Probably courtesy of the cook, whose baking creations Penny had praised extensively. The perfect consolation after the dreadful dinner experience with Arthur Zauner.

Penny flopped down on the bed, grabbed the tiny silver fork, and began to gorge herself on the cake. It tasted even more delicious than it looked.

When she had already devoured half the piece, it occurred to her that a cup of hot chocolate would be the crowning glory for this late-night sin. She was tired and had little desire to leave her bed again, but it couldn't be helped. The thought of hot chocolate with that lovely cake was just too tempting. She could almost taste it in her mouth.

Penny left the room and ran down the stairs to the ground floor. Nothing was stirring in the old house, all the inhabitants seemed to be asleep already. However, as she headed for the kitchen, she noticed a sliver of light coming from under the door. Cautiously, she peeked into the room, not wanting to run into Arthur Zauner again, who might be treating himself to a late-night drink. No hot chocolate in the world was worth having another argument with that creep.

But Penny could breathe a sigh of relief. It was only Emma, the cook, who was still at work in the kitchen. She was sorting cutlery into a drawer—and winced with a sharp cry when Penny entered the room.

"Sorry," Penny said. "I didn't mean to scare you." She ran over to the refrigerator and grabbed a carton of milk. "I just want to make myself a quick cup of hot chocolate to go with that lovely lemon cake you brought to my room."

Emma stepped in her path. "Why don't you let me do that? You are a guest in this house. No, don't argue." She took the milk carton from Penny's hand and began rummaging in one of the cupboards, probably looking for cocoa powder.

Penny thanked the eager cook, then—condemned to temporary inactivity—settled down at the large table in the center of the kitchen.

Reclining on her chair, she noticed that the room seemed to be spinning around her all of a sudden. A dizzy spell?

She hadn't been asleep yet, and she wasn't really that exhausted. Or was she?

Suddenly there was this burn in her stomach—and now that she registered it, she found that her palate felt the same. It was an abrupt pain, as if she had eaten a handful of hot chili peppers. Startled, she gasped for breath.

Emma put a tiny pot on the stove and brought the milk to a boil. "I'm glad you like the cake," she said, gazing at Penny over her shoulder. "It's one of my own favorites, too. But it wasn't me who brought it to your room. I guess someone else wanted to please you."

Penny lifted her head with a jolt, which only added to the dizziness. "What was that?" she asked, in a tone that startled Emma.

"Are you all right, Penny?" the cook replied anxiously. "Did I say something wrong?"

Penny's tongue felt dry and got stuck to the roof of her mouth, while the burning in her stomach grew more violent with each passing minute. She jumped to her feet.

"Excuse me, Emma, I just remembered I have to take care of something," she managed to say. Her mouth was suddenly feeling so parched that even speaking was difficult.

No doubt, something was wrong. But she didn't let the cook know that. She tried to put on a relaxed smile, then said, "I have to leave. Sorry about the hot chocolate, I'll make my own later. Or tomorrow morning."

And with that, she scurried out of the kitchen. She crossed the hall and stumbled up the stairs to her room, where she grabbed her cell phone and purse. The dizziness grew stronger, her stomach burning now like a blaze.

Fortunately, there was a cab rank just around the corner

from Villa Schümann. Hopefully there'd be a taxi waiting there—that would be faster than calling an ambulance. As Penny hurried back down the stairs and out of the house, her mind was running amok.

Poison, poison, poison! She didn't know which one, but the symptoms weren't boding well.

The lemon cake! The cook had baked it, but it had not been her who'd taken the generous piece to Penny's room.

Fortunately, two cabs were waiting at the stand. Penny staggered into the back seat of the first car. "The nearest hospital. Please hurry," she blurted out. Her throat now seemed to be ablaze as well. Every word was hurting like a pinprick.

Fortunately, the cab driver was quick on the uptake. He gave Penny a glance in the rearview mirror, his eyes widened, then he started the engine and stepped on the gas.

The hospital was an old facility, dating back to the nineteenth century—like so many other structures here in the district. The individual clinics were housed in several different buildings, scattered like bungalows in a large park.

The cab driver kept following the signs toward the emergency department at a brisk speed. On arrival, he came to a screeching halt in the middle of the driveway. He helped Penny out of the car, and the next thing she knew, he was dragging her into the building.

She was on the verge of losing consciousness, noticing only dimly they were entering some sort of reception room, where a male nurse immediately rushed to their aid. His eyes also widened in alarm as he glanced at Penny.

Not good at all, she thought. Then suddenly everything went dark around her.

14

"Good morning," said a woman's voice. It sounded friendly but also somehow stern. It seemed to come from far away.

Penny opened her eyes. Or rather, she tried to. Her eyelids wouldn't do her bidding. She had to blink a few times before she was able see anything. Then, however, she recognized a sober, very small hospital room. It had only one window, overlooking the old trees of a park.

She was lying on a narrow bed, with its head slightly inclined. Behind her back were two firm pillows that held her half upright. *You're at the hospital*, Penny reminded herself. *You've been poisoned*!

But from the looks of it, she had survived. The walls still seemed a little shaky, but her stomach was no longer burning like the fires of hell. Her mouth, however, was completely parched. The woman who had just woken her— probably a doctor—sat down on the edge of the bed and handed Penny a glass of water.

"You've been lucky," the woman said as Penny greedily emptied the glass. "Damn lucky. Things could have taken a very different turn, despite our best efforts. I hope this will teach you not to get involved in such stupid experiments! It's none of my business, but you're not a teenager anymore!"

Penny tried to pull herself up on her elbows so she could sit completely upright. She only succeeded on the second try. What was the doctor talking about? Stupid experiments?

"I don't understand," she said cautiously.

The doctor frowned. "Oh, don't do that, will you? Do you think you can fool me? Cantharidin—the oil beetle's poison. Did some cool guy pitch it to you as an aphrodisiac? A hot night you won't soon forget? Well, I think you've accomplished that."

"Wait, what are you saying? What kind of poison? I certainly didn't volunteer to—"

Penny bit her tongue. If she'd claim to be the victim of an assassination attempt then the doctor needed to get the police involved. Was that a good idea? Her mind started to work feverishly, while the stern medic was giving her a surprised look.

An attempt on her life, at the Schümanns' home. As frightening as the incident was, it finally gave Penny the proof she had been looking for: Niní's death had not been an accident. It was murder! Why else would someone try to get rid of a troublesome detective? And in such a drastic way.

Should she take Niní Delight's case back to the police in light of this new development?

It would put an end to—or at least hinder—her own investigations. And the murderer would be warned that they now knew of his existence. He would learn that his poison attempt on Penny had almost succeeded.

This had to be avoided at all costs!

Until now, no one at Villa Schümann knew what had happened to Penny. Only Emma had seen her last night right after the attack, and Penny had not given any explanation for her rather abrupt departure from the house.

The murderer had no way of knowing whether she had eaten his poisoned cake. He wouldn't have been reckless enough to sneak into her room during the hours of the night, in order to check if he'd succeeded in finishing her off. And now it was still early morning. If she returned to the house quickly and secured the remainders of the cake, the killer would never know what had taken place.

No, the police were out of the question. At least for now. The officers wouldn't be able to investigate the case from within, so to speak—by joining the family in their own house and mingling with Niní's friends, like Penny had done. They certainly could not make any better progress. At least, that's what Penny told herself. Later, as soon as she'd have a concrete lead and needed help, she could always call them in.

Of course, it was a reckless thing to do. Maybe even foolish. The same could be said about her whole new—self-styled—role as a security consultant. But she loved her job! And she was good at what she did. She'd prove that to this poisoner! *She* had to catch this killer. Now that he had attacked her personally, she owed it to herself.

But she had to be damn careful! Obviously, this bastard had no qualms about getting rid of her in the most radical way. And apparently, arsenic wasn't the only poison he knew how to use.

She was still very much in the dark, but the circle of suspects had become really manageable now. Poisoning a piece of Emma's cake and placing it next to Penny's bed— no outsider could be responsible for that. Only someone who knew his way around Villa Schümann could have been responsible. Just like for the murder of Niní.

Yes, murder. She knew that now.

And you particularly like Alex as co-investigator, don't you? the voice of her conscience spoke up. *Isn't that another reason why you're so keen to pursue the case yourself?*

Quickly she directed her thoughts in another, more innocuous direction. Who had been in the house last night and had had the opportunity to take the poisoned cake to her room? It shouldn't be too difficult to find out. On the other hand, the cake could have been placed there earlier in the afternoon. She hadn't entered her guest room all day. *Bummer.*

"Ms. Küfer?" The doctor's voice brought her back to the present. To her hospital bed. Apparently, the woman had asked her a question. In any case, she was now looking expectantly at Penny.

"I'm sorry, what did you say?" muttered Penny, lost in thought.

The doctor's eyes narrowed. "I asked you whether you've been attacked. You said you didn't ingest the poison voluntarily. Which I'd assumed. Oil beetles are a fairly popular alternative to Spanish fly in our latitudes. That's why I'd assumed ..."

"That I'd been playing around with substance abuse for a bit?" Penny completed the sentence for her.

Spanish fly? she repeated in her mind. She'd heard of that before. It was actually a popular party drug, if you wanted to put it that way. One that was said to increase sexual desire. *Oh great.* She did her best to look guilty and contrite.

"So, have you been playing around?" the doctor asked.

"Well, not quite consciously," Penny replied vaguely. "It was actually just an, uh, little game with a friend. Maybe he was trying to play a joke on me—or give me a particularly potent dose. But it was definitely an accident!"

She had never heard of this *oil beetle* before, but she could catch up on that later. First, she had to escape the clutches of her lifesaver. As well-meaning as this doctor certainly was.

"An accident?" the woman hissed. "You could have died, for God's sake! Haven't you figured that out yet? We should press charges against this so-called friend of yours!"

"Oh no, that's not a good idea," Penny said quickly. She tried hard to put on the most innocent puppy look. At once rueful and pitiful. "It...is complicated," she added.

Her head was still a little foggy, but she had to make an effort to think clearly now and convince this doctor that no further steps were necessary. Especially not a report to the police.

"I'm sorry," she muttered, "I'm sure it won't happen again. No more experiments, I promise you. But please don't press charges." She topped it off with another puppy look.

The doctor shook her head in exasperation, but then she seemed to relent and put on a half-sympathetic smile.

Penny grinned back gratefully. "Can you release me already? I'm feeling very well, and I, uh, have an urgent appointment this morning."

The doctor stood up and glanced at the chart hanging at the foot of Penny's bed. Apparently she wanted to check certain readings that would tell her the extent to which Penny had actually recovered.

Then she nodded. "As far as I'm concerned, you're out of danger. And you do seem to have a strong constitution. But take it easy, will you?"

Penny nodded quickly. "I promise." She certainly had no intention of being poisoned again!

15

Penny's knees were still a little wobbly when she unlocked the front gate of Villa Schümann with her guest key. She headed straight for the stairs and climbed them as quickly as she could. She had to get to her room and secure the leftover cake. First, she didn't want the killer to learn that she'd actually swallowed his poison bait and now knew of his existence. And second, she wanted to have the remains of the cake analyzed to see if they actually contained the oil beetle's poison. What had the doctor called it? *Cantharidin*. Too bad that such analyses required a laboratory, which Penny did not have.

When she turned into the corridor at the top of the stairs that led to her room, she stopped abruptly. Because in that very instant she caught sight of Alex Adamas—who was just slipping out of her guest room!

"What are you doing here?" she snapped before it occurred to her to say good morning first.

He put on a guilty expression. "Sorry. I'd knocked. I thought you'd be in and just hadn't heard me. I was just checking on you."

He looked genuinely concerned. "Is everything all right with you?" he asked. "Emma mentioned you'd stormed out of the house in the middle of the night. And that you seemed to be sick. What happened?"

Penny struggled with herself for a moment. A far too brief

moment. Then she decided to take Alex into her confidence. Never mind that she'd resolved—barely an hour ago—not to tell anyone about the attempt on her life.

She could not trust Alex, was not allowed to! She hardly knew this man, and he was one of the suspects. One of an ever-shrinking circle of suspects!

But she *wanted to* trust him, there was no denying that. "Follow your instincts," one of her instructors at the detective academy had been fond of preaching. "But don't forget your gun."

"Come on in," was all she said, pushing Alex into her room and closing the door behind her. Her eyes fell on the nightstand—on the plate with the leftover cake, which was still in the same place where she had left it at night.

"Hey Penny," Alex exclaimed, "you didn't finish your cake. Don't let Emma find out about that! Lemon cake is one of her absolute specialties."

Penny winced as if thunderstruck. "Did you bring me this cake, Alex?"

"Me? No. Didn't you get it from of the kitchen yourself?"

Penny shook her head wordlessly. Then she added, barely audibly, "Do you think it possible that Emma brought it to my room?"

Alex grinned. "She must have really taken you into her heart to do something like that. Anyway, my advice is to get rid of the leftovers before Paula cleans up your room. If she takes the plate back to the kitchen like that, you're guaranteed to piss Emma off."

Alex made himself comfortable on the edge of the bed

and reached for the plate. "I'll help you," he said with a mischievous grin. "I love this cake. Oh, you even got frosting on top. That's new –"

"No!" exclaimed Penny as he tried to bring a piece of cake to his mouth. With a jerky hand movement, she knocked the cake fork from his fingers.

Alex looked at her in alarm, "Hey, sorry! I thought you weren't going to finish the cake."

Penny couldn't take it anymore. Was Valerie's fiancé putting on a full-blown show for her? Or was he really as completely clueless and innocent as he pretended to be?

"The cake is poisoned," she said straightforwardly, staring Alex right into the face. She wanted to see his reaction. Maybe that would tell her if he was lying. Or just how gifted he was at acting?

"What?" he croaked. He looked so startled that he seemed to miss a heartbeat.

Penny nodded vigorously. "I'm pretty sure the poison was in the cake. Maybe even in the frosting, if that's not usually part of the recipe. The killer may have added it."

She took the plate from Alex's hand and scrutinized the icing. It looked like frosting; maybe it even was frosting...just prepared with a little oil beetle poison.

She gave Alex a full report of her stay in the hospital. Repeated the doctor's words for him.

He was either an accomplished actor or her story completely surprised—no, shocked—him.

"An attempt on your life, here in the house!?" he moaned.

"You know what that means," Penny said.

He sat there paralyzed for a moment, then sprang to his feet and pulled her into his arms. "Oh God, thank goodness you're okay!"

The next moment he let go of her, while Penny couldn't help but enjoy the afterglow of his warmth, breathing in the scent of his skin.

She shook her head, trying to get rid of the unwelcome feeling that had taken possession of her.

Alex didn't seem to notice what was going on with her. "So Niní's death really wasn't a suicide," he said quietly.

"I guess we can take that as a given now," Penny replied.

He pulled his cell phone out of his pocket and began swiping across the screen. "I've never heard of this oil bug," he said. "You?"

He was now back in Watson mode, that much was obvious. His snooping instincts came to the fore.

You'd rather have enjoyed more of his care, huh? the inner voice that represented Penny's conscience piped up.

"Cantharidin, the poison of the oil beetle, is ten times more poisonous than strychnine," he read aloud. "Good God!"

A cold shiver ran down her spine. Compared to this poison, of which she'd never heard before, arsenic suddenly seemed really homely. Who in the Villa Schümann had a knowledge of killer beetles? Penny would have loved to claim that she had sensed the poisoner's trap...because she was such an excellent detective. But nothing more than her weakness for hot chocolate had saved her life. If she'd eaten the whole piece of cake, she probably wouldn't have made it to the hospital alive.

She carried the plate with the leftovers to one of the cupboards, opened the door, and wanted to place it on the top shelf. Where no one, who wasn't looking for it, would find it so easily.

"What are you doing?" asked Alex.

"I want to get the remains analyzed," Penny explained. "So far, all we have is the doctor's word on this oil beetle poisoning. But I have to find a suitable lab first and come up with a harmless story as to why there's poison in this cake."

"That won't be necessary," Alex said. "I know just the woman for the job. My Aunt Henry!"

"Henry? *Aunt*?"

Alex smiled. "She's...well, a little eccentric. And she can't stand her given name. Henrietta. But as far as lab work goes, she's a genius. Or rather I should say, she's a genius in all kinds of fields. She works in pharmaceutical research, and microbes are her professional specialty. But she knows every substance in the world, it seems to me. Poisonous animals and deadly plants are one of her hobbies."

"Nice way to pass the time," said Penny, who felt instant sympathy for Alex's aunt.

"I'll take the cake to her, if you like," Alex said. "That way, we'll have a reliable result in no time. After all, I'm Aunt Henry's favorite nephew, you know. She'll do anything for me. Otherwise, she's rather the recluse. Spends more time in her lab than in her apartment."

"Then she must have taken a special shine to you," Penny

said.

Alex twisted the corners of his mouth into the mischievous smile that by now seemed so familiar to Penny. "Well, to me—and my gems," he said. "The only worldly pleasure she likes to indulge in. She collects rubies and sapphires."

"Then she's wealthy too, the lucky woman?"

Alex shrugged. "I'm sure she is. Although she doesn't care about money. But I'm sure her company pays her a princely salary. Even though Auntie is researching stuff that might not see mass production before the twenty-second century. If ever."

"I'd love to meet her, your Aunt Henry," Penny said. "Maybe she can really help us with the cake."

Alex frowned. "If it's all right with you, I'd rather meet her on my own. Otherwise, I'd have to explain why I'm acquainted with a detective and how there might be a murderer on the loose in this house. Aunt Henry is a little—how shall I put it—well, paranoid you could say. If I let her in on the truth, she'll start spinning the wildest conspiracy theories. I'll have to come up with some white lie about why this cake might be poisoned."

"All right," Penny said. "When do you think you'll be able to meet her?"

Alex was swiping across his cell phone again. Obviously, he was checking his schedule.

"Nothing that can't be postponed," he muttered. "What's buying rare pearls compared to a murder hunt!" He spoke in a quippy tone, and his expression seemed almost euphoric. He was clearly delighted to be playing Watson again.

"But not a word to anyone about this incident, okay?" Penny put him under oath.

16

Right after Alex had disappeared, Penny dug her own cell out of her purse. She looked up the number for Christy Schelling, a young detective who had been in training with her.

Christy had landed a job as an assistant at one of the city's most prestigious detective agencies less than two weeks after graduating from the detective academy. Penny had not succeeded, although she had also sent out numerous applications. But she did not envy Christy's brilliant career start. What she had found for herself—hunting murderers, albeit in a certain gray area of the law—was so much better!

Today was a holiday, but Penny couldn't take that into account. Time was of the essence. If Christy didn't answer the phone, she would leave her a message. But female detectives—and young, ambitious ones at that—didn't care about holidays! Criminals didn't take weekends off either.

Christy answered the phone right after the second ring. And after the two young detectives had made minimal small talk, Penny got right down to business: "Can you do some surveillance for me, Christy? And a background check? As thorough as possible." She passed on to her young colleague the scanty data she had gathered so far on Lars Simon—not least with Alex's help. "I need everything and anything on him, okay?" she told Christy. "As soon as possible, please. Call in a colleague if you like."

Lucinda would certainly not mind the expense. Now that Penny had flushed out Niní's murderer, there was no time to lose. Penny didn't want to give the killer the opportunity to carry out another attack on her life.

Did Lars Simon, that faithless lover of Niní's who'd so quickly consoled himself with a new girlfriend after Niní's tragic death, have something to do with the poisoned cake in Penny's room? It was not impossible to sneak into Villa Schümann unseen, yet this idea seemed quite far-fetched. Besides, Lars could hardly be the mysterious A—Niní's great love. Had he murdered her anyway?

Well, if there were dark secrets lurking in his past, Christy would bring them to light. Penny had full confidence in her colleague's abilities.

She herself opened her laptop after the phone call and navigated again to the website of the so-called heart whisperer. That sorceress in love matters, who had allegedly helped Niní to find the proof of love—the card of her beloved. By casting a spell!

Penny had only briefly glanced at this heart whisperer's online services in Saskia's office. Now she took a more systematic look at the site.

Everything that was on offer revolved around love magic. However, there was no online store with off-the-shelf products or services. Each customer was individually advised and cared for, if you wanted to believe the website's full-bodied promises. Prices upon request.

Supposedly, the love witch worked with real magic forces, claiming such power was inherent in all women. *Magic is our birthright, which we have only forgotten,* was the core message. *With my help, you can reclaim what has always been yours.*

Customer reviews were numerous and downright euphoric.

Penny had to get in touch with this woman. Perhaps this self-styled witch did know valuable details about Niní's affairs of the heart that could be elicited from her.

However, there was neither a street address nor a phone number to be found on the website—the typical online business of the modern age. The only available option to get in touch was a chat window that popped up in the lower right corner of the screen. A photo of the heart whisperer was displayed, along with the question: "How can I help you?"

Penny scrutinized the photograph for a moment. The woman had to be about fifty years old; she was flamboyantly dressed up, with flashy make-up, a kind of hair band with glittering stones and, in addition, huge earrings that looked like diamonds but were probably just costume jewelry. A modern sorceress just as one might imagine her. Not that Penny had too much experience with such service providers.

The chat window required you to enter your name, then, in the next step, you could write a message.

Penny pondered for a moment, then typed: *Penelope.* She never used that name, not even on her business cards. Wherever she went, whomever she met, she always gave her name as just Penny. But here in this chat window she wanted to reveal as little of herself as possible for the time being. She didn't plan to come out as a detective either – that would certainly make the heart whisperer shut up rather than talk.

A very happy client of yours has recommended you to me, she typed into the box. The heart whisperer would certainly want to have a conversation with an auspicious new client. Penny hoped to arrange a personal meeting, even though the witch usually seemed to perform her magic strictly online. *My case is real difficult,* she added in the chat window. *Would an in-person appointment be possible on short notice?*

While getting to know each other better and chatting for a bit, Penny would casually mention that Niní was the one who had recommended the witch. Then she would address the success with the love message Niní had received from the man of her dreams. Thanks to the heart whisperer's spell. "How did you do that?" Penny would ask with an innocent look in her eyes, gazing admiringly at the witch. "I wish I could achieve something similar!"

Yes, that sounded like a reasonable strategy to hopefully learn everything the heart whisperer knew about Niní's love problems.

Penny clicked SEND, then closed the laptop. Did the heart whisperer also work on holidays? Hopefully. Then one could perhaps count on an answer today.

Now that all urgent matters had been taken care of, Penny's gaze fell on the inviting double bed that dominated her 'operations center' at the Schümann home. It was looking all but irresistible right now. She might have survived the poison attack well, but she still felt a little queasy. Her energy level was low, and a short nap was just the thing she needed...

First, however, she walked over to the door and turned the key in the lock. For the next few hours, she could gladly do without any visitors harboring sinister intentions.

17

The ringing of the phone jolted Penny from her sleep. She fumbled for her cell she had left on the nightstand. What time was it, anyway?

She blinked at the display. Afternoon already? The caller was Lucinda Schümann. Penny picked up, trying not to sound too sleepy.

Lucinda got right to the point: "I'd like to talk to you, Penny. Could you stop by my place this afternoon?"

"No problem," Penny said. "I'm in your house anyway."

Ten minutes later, she was sitting opposite her client in Lucinda's *porcelain room*. The walls were adorned by artfully painted plates, and cute little figurines were arranged on the shelves. Shepherds, nymphs, dancers and flute players. A bourgeois idyll straight out of the Biedermeier era—and thus quite a contrast in style to the rest of the house, dominated by Art Nouveau.

Mrs. Schümann seemed very distant. She didn't look Penny in the eye but fixed her gaze on some figurine on the shelf next to them.

"How is the investigation going?" she began without much enthusiasm in her voice. She didn't mention the attack on Penny with a single word. Alex seemed to have kept quiet about it, as he had promised.

"I'm following up on some leads," Penny said. It was necessary to keep even her client in the dark about the status of the investigation—not that one word too many would end up reaching the killer's ears.

"Nothing concrete yet?" asked Lucinda, again avoiding Penny's gaze.

"You'll have to give me some time, Mrs. Schümann. I've only been working on this case for four days." Penny shot her client a friendly smile. "I'll do my best, but you can't expect any miracles." She let her smile grow even wider.

"Yes, yes, sure. I understand," said Mrs. Schümann. Something was on her mind, that much was obvious.

"You, as my client, should be upfront with me," Penny encouraged her. "Is there something I need to know? "

"Oh, it's just...no, that won't do. I can't keep it from you anyway." Lucinda paused for a moment, took a deep breath, then blurted out, "Arthur thinks I'm a fool to have hired you! He says I'm just not coping with Nini's death and am deluding myself. He claims the police clearly proved it was suicide."

"I understand," Penny said slowly. Arthur Zauner, getting in her way again. No surprise, really.

Lucinda continued, "As sorry as I am, Arthur no longer wants you in the house. I guess he doesn't see you a professional detective. He thinks you're just wasting my money. And he's a lawyer, he must know about such things. We're going to be married, very soon. Anyway, that's my wish. To enjoy our sunset years together. That's why I don't think you should...should make any further inquiries."

Lucinda took a deep breath. She was visibly relieved that the words had now been spoken.

Penny's smile faded. She pondered for a moment about how to respond. She couldn't let Lucinda fire her. Not now that she finally knew Niní's death had been an insidiously planned murder.

If she was kicked out of the house, the murderer would get away with his crime. She couldn't let that happen. So she had no choice but to tell Lucinda Schümann the truth.

"I understand your concerns," Penny began cautiously, "and the importance you place on the word of your, um, significant other...but he's wrong. Your daughter *was* murdered. By someone who's a regular in your house. Or even lives here," she added bluntly. "The same person tried to poison me last night."

Lucinda Schümann gave a yelp, then slapped her hand over her mouth and stared at Penny, aghast. "You can't be serious! Poison? How...did that happen?"

Penny still couldn't be one hundred percent sure whether the poison had really been in the icing of the cake. Hence, she only replied: "I was served a dish that was prepared with the poison of the oil beetle. This probably won't mean anything to you, but—" She stopped short.

Lucinda had suddenly turned very pale and let out a gasp, as if Penny's words had given her a terrible fright. She put her hand to her throat. "The poison of the *oil beetle*?" she whispered.

"Don't tell me you know this insect?" Penny asked in surprise.

"I..." That's all Lucinda could say. She seemed visibly confused, an agonizing battle raging inside her.

"Mrs. Schümann?" Penny said gently. "Do you remember our very first conversation? In your winter garden? At that time, you told me that you trusted my mother's judgment one hundred percent. She'd recommended me to you. I know you probably trust Arthur even more, but believe me, a lawyer is no expert in solving murder cases. I can't claim to be the best detective on the planet either, but I swear to you that I'll do my utmost. I will find your daughter's killer. You have my word on that. But you have to trust me and let me do my job! This attack on me shows that I've gotten very close to the killer. He no longer feels safe to get away with Niní's murder. We must stay on the case, and you need to talk to me, okay? Now, what about the oil beetle?"

Lucinda swallowed hard a few times. She stared over at her porcelain figurines, then back at Penny. She began to knead her hands in her lap. But eventually she did regain her composure. "There was...an incident. With the gardener. A few weeks ago." Lucinda's voice sounded as if she were speaking from beyond the grave. "Nothing that seemed significant to me at the time. But now..."

Penny gave her an encouraging nod, "Tell me about it."

"Our gardener. Robbie. Arthur caught him collecting bugs in the garden instead of going about his work. He confronted him. That's when Robbie showed him the bugs – he called them oil bugs, I'm sure of it. I happened to be nearby and joined them because I wanted to know what the problem was. Robbie claimed wholeheartedly that an extraordinary sexual enhancer could be obtained from this creature. And then he actually had the cheek to ask Arthur if he didn't want some of it, too. That's when Arthur fired him."

"Oil bugs as a sexual enhancer?" Penny repeated incredulously. But then she remembered what the doctor at the hospital had said. That the oil beetle was a relative of the Spanish fly, which had been used for centuries as a popular aphrodisiac. Not much different from a sexual enhancer.

"Robbie swore by the bugs," Lucinda said. "But he warned to be careful, too. *Too much of it, and a man will never enjoy love's pleasures again.* His words were something like that. Of course, Arthur didn't continue the conversation. And neither did I. Robbie left us that very day."

An eerie silence fell over the room. For a few minutes, the two women sat together in silence. Penny was lost in dark thoughts, while Lucinda stared at her hands, which she was still kneading in her lap.

Finally, Penny spoke up again. "Was anyone else present at this incident in the garden, besides you and Arthur?" she asked.

Lucida shook her head. Her neck suddenly seemed very stiff.

"There's something else I wanted to ask you," Penny continued after another pause. "I'm still trying to establish the alibis of all the possible suspects on the day Niní died. That's routine in a case like this, no matter how unlikely some people may seem as perpetrators."

"Yes?" murmured Lucinda.

"Well. As far as Arthur's alibi is concerned, I still need confirmation. Maybe you can help me there."

Lucinda looked at Penny with wide eyes, but she didn't protest. The matter of the oil beetle still seemed to be tormenting her.

"Arthur claimed he had been reading in the library at the time in question," Penny said. "All day long. Did you perhaps see him there?"

"All day?" Lucinda echoed. All of a sudden, she was looking even more confused.

Penny got worried. Her client was going to have a heart attack if they went on like this. She had to give Lucinda some rest and continue the conversation at a later time.

But Mrs. Schümann took the floor: "Arthur *was* in the library early in the morning. That's when I saw him. A few hours later, I wanted to stop by again 'cause I wanted to ask him something."

She fell silent. Her eyes started wandering over a few tiny blue and white porcelain plates on the wall. She looked as if she no longer knew where she was.

"Go on?" Penny probed cautiously.

"I couldn't find Arthur anywhere," whispered Mrs. Schümann.

Penny let a few moments pass. Lucinda was breathing hard. Just one more question, and she would leave the poor woman alone. "Did you check with Arthur later to find out where he'd been?"

Mrs. Schümann shook her head. "No. I don't want to be one of those women who try to control their husbands' every move. Arthur hates that sort of thing; he's very independent."

She cleared her throat and straightened her back. "I'm sure he just made a dash to the office. Or he was running an errand."

"Yeah, probably," Penny said, trying to put on a reassuring smile.

Then she rose and gently put her hand on Lucinda's shoulder. "Get some rest, will you? I'll be in touch again as soon as I have any news for you."

Lucinda nodded. "Thank you," she whispered, barely audible.

Penny wasn't going to be fired—for now. She had gained some time and perhaps discovered an important new puzzle piece in the murder case. Arthur Zauner. It was all too easy to imagine this man as a ruthless killer.

No jumping to conclusions, Penny admonished herself. Sometimes it was hard to remember this important principle.

18

In the evening of the same day, Valerie was doing another rehearsal for her new show, and the same audience as two days before had gathered at Villa Schümann. Or rather: all except Alex Adamas. Valerie's fiancé was conspicuous by his absence, but that didn't seem to bother her.

This time the small group had gathered for dinner right in the ballroom because it was raining outside. Penny joined Tony, Saskia and Valerie at the table as Paula was serving aperitifs. Dinner was presented buffet style this time, which was just fine with Penny. She didn't eat from any dish that several of the others dinner guests hadn't already tasted.

Of course, that was a bit paranoid—the killer would hardly go so far as to poison entire food platters and thus kill people indiscriminately. But better safe than sorry. As a drink, she took only water from a carafe that stood on the table, so everyone could help themselves. All in all, she ate and drank very little. Her stomach was not yet in the mood for a feast again.

As inconspicuously as possible, she inquired where the other three people present at table had spent last night. She had to find out who'd had the opportunity to poison her cake.

Valerie confirmed what Alex had said about her last night: she had been plagued by a headache and had gone to bed early. Alex, however, had not been with her to really testify to that. He had, after all, spent several hours with Penny in the garden. So Valerie had no alibi.

The situation was no better for Saskia or Tony. Both gave unhelpful answers. A relaxed evening in front of the TV or, in Saskia's case, a good book, something to eat, then gone to bed alone. Almost the same statement, twice. Shouldn't these young, creative, and successful people be hanging out at glittering parties and celebrating life to the fullest?

Where was Alex Adamas tonight, Penny wondered? Had he gotten an appointment with Aunt Henry? Was he out and about in his role as her Watson?

As if he could read her thoughts, Tony, who was sitting to her right, suddenly asked: "Where is Valerie's Prince Charming tonight? He won't want to miss the show, will he?"

And Valerie promptly gave the answer Penny wanted to hear, "He's visiting his aunt—thankfully without me. She scares me."

"Something scares you?" asked Tony, raising his eyebrows in a teasing manner.

Valerie smiled. "This aunt is a mixture of witch and alchemist. Her house is a chamber of horrors, and God only knows what she's growing and experimenting with in her lab."

With those words, Valerie abruptly turned her head and addressed Penny, "Can we talk for a minute? After the show? Will you wait for me?"

"Oh, how mysterious," Tony commented. Then suddenly

Saskia jumped to her feet and urged Valerie to try on one of the new costumes she had sewn herself. "I lack Niní's visionary creativity, of course," she said, a bit too solemnly for Penny's taste. "But see if you like it."

Valerie insisted on getting dessert from the buffet first, but then everyone got to work.

The rehearsal dragged on endlessly. Nevertheless, Penny enjoyed the enchanted atmosphere in the magnificent old ballroom, with its stucco decorations, countless mirrors and dimmed lights. Valerie's look, her dresses and lace lingerie reminiscent of vaudeville dancers from long ago, reinforced the impression one gained in this almost magical place: that one had fallen through time, two to three generations into the past.

The different acts Valerie was rehearsing were at the same time a bit old-fashioned, yet very erotic. The new show would certainly be a great success.

Still, the young diva seemed unfocused tonight. Tony kept nagging her, and Penny couldn't shake the feeling that a dark cloud was hanging over the house. Pure imagination, of course. At most the people in the grand old hall were a bit anxious. Losing their nerve.

Were they afraid of the murderer in their midst, of whose existence they couldn't even know? Or was one of them—or even several—feeling nervous because they themselves were behind the attack on Penny and now had to fear being exposed?

Saskia kept scurrying about to help Valerie change between the different acts, but in between she took a seat next to Penny and made an attentive spectator.

At one point though, she suddenly turned to Penny and asked, "So, did you find the mysterious card? The love greeting from Niní's dream man?"

"Not yet," Penny lied. She couldn't take all and sundry into her confidence. Having Alex as her sidekick in the investigation was unprofessional enough.

Before Saskia could think of drilling further, Penny countered with a question of a her own. "Say, how did Niní actually come across this heart whisperer? Do you remember?"

Saskia seemed to think hard for a while. Then she said, "I think a friend recommended her to Niní. One who'd found her Mister Right with the help of this love witch. Something like that. Can't remember the name of the friend though. I must confess I always listened to Niní with only half an ear on these subjects. She often started talking about it right in the middle of some work project when my head was full of business. Hmm, was it Valerie, perhaps? No, I think it was a friend. I really don't remember. Sorry."

"That's all right, thank you," Penny said.

19

When Tony and Saskia finally said their goodbyes, leaving Penny alone with Valerie, the burlesque diva dropped exhausted onto a chair. She began massaging her perfectly formed legs, which had to be aching after all the lascivious bouncing around of the evening.

Penny sat down next to her and looked at her encouragingly. "What did you want to talk to me about?"

Valerie frowned. She chewed on her lip for a moment, but the next instant she launched into it, "Lucinda told me about the conversation you two were having this afternoon. She's very upset, completely unsettled about Arthur. You've got her all rattled."

"I'm sorry about that, but—"

Valerie waved it off. "That's all right. I must confess, I wouldn't mind in the least if you talked her out of this Arthur. Does that make me a bad daughter?" She shrugged. "But as for his alibi on the day of Niní's death—no, Niní's murder it must be called now—oh, God, how awful!"

Valerie's darkly made-up eyes widened. "So there's something I haven't told Lucinda, but you should know. I'm loathe to talk about our dirty little family secrets in public, but I think I can count on your discretion, right?"

"Of course," Penny said, trying hard to mask her surprise.

"So...I know where Arthur was on that day," Valerie continued. "Around lunchtime, anyway. He was seen. He was with a woman, meeting her at a café."

"Don't tell me now he's having an affair?" Penny interrupted. Arthur, the moralizer-in-chief?

"No. That would be too good to be true, wouldn't it? The woman he met is a lawyer, probably a colleague of his. However, she specializes in family law, while he's mostly focused on real estate and such. The meeting was a consultation. Arthur wanted to know how Lucinda could best disinherit her children—meaning Niní and me. He inquired about legal options and obstacles. And how he should best pitch the idea to Lucinda."

Penny stared at Valerie. "What a bastard!" she exclaimed. Very unprofessional on her part, but Valerie didn't seem to have heard the remark at all.

"How come you know all this, if you don't mind me asking?" inquired Penny.

Valerie hesitated. "I...called in a professional colleague of yours. A private investigator."

Penny wanted to say something back, but Valerie wouldn't let her get a word in. "Wait, I know how this sounds. But please believe me that I didn't make it easy on myself. I gave Arthur every chance in the beginning. I was super hopeful when Lucinda told us that there was this new man in her life. And so was Niní. Our mother had been alone for a very long time after our dad's death."

Penny nodded sympathetically but remained in the listening role.

Valerie continued, "In the beginning, Lucy always met with Arthur in some other place than our house. We didn't get to see him at all for the first few months. Niní and I assumed that Mama was worried about whether we would accept him. But in truth, it was about whether *he* would accept *us*!"

A bitter look came over her flawlessly beautiful face. "Honestly, I wish my mother all the happiness in the world. I know she's crazy about that Arthur, and in his horrible way, maybe he's crazy about her, too. But as for Niní and me—he's been treating us like scum from the very beginning. Even at our very first meeting. I got the impression that he must be a terrible person. And so, I wanted to make sure there wasn't a nasty surprise waiting for Lucy at the end. That's why I hired this detective. A background check...that's what he called it. And that's what I paid him for. I wanted to know if there were any skeletons in Arthur's closet."

"So, are there any?" asked Penny.

Valerie shook her head. "No, but in the course of his surveillance, the detective recorded Arthur's meeting with that lawyer friend of his. Complete with video and audio. It's amazing what can be done these days. My private eye spied on the two of them at the coffeehouse, and they didn't notice a thing."

"When did your detective observe this meeting? Do you remember the exact time?"

"The two were at the coffee house from 12:30 p.m. until a little after 2:00 p.m."

"And after that?"

"Arthur left, heading for our house, and the detective

stopped his surveillance for the day. I didn't order round-the-clock service, of course."

That meant Arthur would have had plenty of time after-wards to poison one of the unwanted daughters, Penny thought. Perhaps the info the family lawyer had given him at the café, about the possibilities of disinheritance, had not been satisfactory...and Arthur had immediately come up with an alternative plan? Murder?

A man like him might have been capable of such a deed. And he definitely had no alibi for the hours before Niní's death. That much was certain now.

Perhaps he had already prepared the murder as plan B? To get rid of the 'fallen' daughters of his future wife—if not by legal means, then by poison. Nowadays, in the Internet age, procuring arsenic—or any of a hundred other poten-tially lethal substances—didn't pose much of a problem.

Arthur was a vile fellow, no question...but such cold-blooded murder? With this kind of base motive? That seemed outrageous, very hard to imagine.

Penny eyed Valerie, who seemed to be lost in her own thoughts. A dark curl had fallen into her face, and she twisted and twirled it with her fingers while her forehead was all wrinkled up.

In this house, snooping seemed to be all the rage, Penny thought. Alex liked to play detective. Valerie had her moth-er's future husband spied on. Lucinda, in turn, called in a private investigator to solve her daughter's supposed sui-cide. Clearly, there was a greatly increased need for intel in this house.

But that was not why Niní had died. Or was it? Had she possibly been snooping around, too, and found out more than was good for her?

Penny pondered some more. If Niní's death had indeed been the consequence of Arthur Zauner's conversation with the family lawyer, then Valerie was in mortal danger as well.

Was Penny supposed to warn her? *Don't eat or drink anything you didn't prepare yourself?* In a household where an in-house cook took care of the meals, that was probably rather unrealistic.

It was equally impossible for Penny to keep an eye on Valerie around the clock. She couldn't be on her neck, follow her around every step of the way, without it being noticeable.

Would the killer strike again while Penny was in the house? The answer was obvious, and she didn't like it one bit. The killer had not even hesitated to make an attempt on her life.

She had to be on her guard. She confined herself to issuing a general warning to Valerie. "We now know there's an assassin in our midst," she said, "and that he's adept with other poisons too, more exotic ones than arsenic. But we're still in the dark as to why Niní had to die. So we all have to be careful, okay?" At least that sounded less frightening than: *you could be his next victim.*

But would this warning be enough to protect Valerie? Wasn't it Penny's duty now to call the police, after all? It was the kind of impossible decision one so often had to make as a private investigator.

She simply had too little to show to the police. A piece of poisoned cake, if the poison had been in the cake at all. What should the officers do about it? Especially when it came to the question of *who* had been behind the attack.

And as far as security was concerned, police detectives could not protect the residents of Villa Schümann any better than Penny was able to. The police specialized in solving crimes *after* they had been committed. Preventing assassinations was not within their power. For that, one needed private security. Bodyguards. Penny considered for a moment bringing in colleagues from that specialty. Would Lucinda agree to that?

Not if Arthur had a say in the matter. And as far as that was concerned, Penny was under no illusions. She might have been able to give her client pause about Arthur's intentions and his true character...but Lucinda loved this man.

No, as much as Penny disliked it, she came to an inevitable conclusion: in the long run, it was impossible to prevent another murder unless the perpetrator was exposed and brought to justice.

If she called the police now, the killer would keep his head down for the duration of the investigation. During this time, he would probably not plan a new attack, but afterwards?

Was it arrogant of her, Penny wondered, to trust her own abilities most in this matter? After all, she had already solved three murder cases. And she would succeed this time too, she was determined to do so! An irrepressible desire was burning in her to personally hunt down this assassin.

Valerie had not interrupted her thoughts, but now Penny noticed that she was looking at her questioningly.

Penny shook off the trepidation as best she could. She put on an optimistic smile... Then she remembered a detail she had wanted to clarify with Valerie. The love witch! She asked Valerie the same question she had already asked Saskia: did she know how Niní had come across this woman? Had Valerie possibly recommended the heart whisperer herself, as Saskia had suggested?

"Me?" asked Valerie with an amused smile. "A love witch? Sorry, but I'm not into that kind of thing. The esoteric, that was Niní's territory. Besides, I think I 'm able to conquer a man without any magical mumbo-jumbo." She winked at Penny with a lascivious blink. "And Niní wouldn't have needed it either." With these words, Valerie rose and took her leave for the night.

For a few minutes, Penny sat in the now completely deserted ballroom, brooding to herself. Only one of the chandeliers was still alight, the rest of the hall was lost in deep shadow. Ominously deep shadow, as it suddenly appeared to Penny.

It was getting late, but Alex still hadn't come home. She caught herself worrying about his safety more than about all the other inhabitants of the house.

20

Penny went to sleep. She locked her bedroom door and checked her pistol in the nightstand drawer.

Don't be afraid to admit that you feel queasy. There is no shame in fear.

These and other thoughts were haunting her as she was tossing and turning in bed. Sleep didn't want to come. The wind was howling around the house, shaking the branches of the old trees. It was crackling and creaking in the wood, and the roof truss of Villa Schümann also joined in the eerie symphony.

Several times Penny woke up, confused by strange dreams. So she must have fallen asleep after all?

At some point, she thought she was hearing the key creak in the lock. That it was turning—all by itself? She had to think of the locked door behind which Niní's body had been found. Was this particularly cunning murderer able to pick locks with the key inserted without leaving any traces? Was he at work right now to break into Penny's room? Armed with a new diabolical poison...

Just a dream, Penny murmured—but then there was a sudden knock at the door. Cautiously at first, then louder.

Not a dream. Someone was there! The murderer?

Drowsy, she jumped out of bed, slipped on a nightgown, and took the gun out of the nightstand. Hiding the gun behind her back, she crept to the door. With a jerk, Penny yanked it open, ready to act if she sensed even the slightest danger.

Alex was standing in front of the door. Handsome as ever, his dark hair a little tousled, a conspiratorial smile on his face. "So sorry to wake you, but I have news!" he announced.

He didn't wait for Penny to invite him in but literally sprinted past her into the room. Dynamic as a young deer.

Penny unobtrusively put away her pistol, then looked down at herself. The nightgown she was wearing was not exactly a creation of lace and silk like Niní had produced. More of the baggy, long shirt type.

Her eyes wandered to Alex, who was dressed in jeans and a casual polo shirt, had slung a bag around his shoulder, and was still holding the keys to the villa's front door in his hand.

"Just got home?" she asked him, although that was pretty obvious. She felt a great, undeniable relief that nothing had happened to him. That he had returned home unharmed.

What nonsense, she scolded herself. Why should he be in danger?

Alex flopped on the edge of the bed, put on a serious face, and announced, "I just came from Aunt Henry's."

She did not miss how his gaze briefly wandered up and down her body. She quickly headed for the bed as well, trying not to get too close to him. She crawled back under the covers to avoid standing in front of him in the worn nightgown. At the same time, she hated this kind of vanity. After all, what did her looks matter? Or the erotic appeal of her night attire?! If there was any relationship between Alex and her, it was purely professional. He was helping with her investigations. That was all.

She forced herself to put on a businesslike smile. "What have you been able to find out, my dear Watson?"

Alex smirked conspiratorially. He seemed to be enjoying this childish Watson game just as much as she was.

"Aunt Henry confirmed the bug poison thing," he said. "It was in the cake—in the frosting, to be exact. If you had eaten the whole piece, you would have ended up in the morgue instead of the hospital. Aunt Henry knows how to be subtle," he added. He furrowed his brow. "What a horrible idea."

Penny nodded silently. What Alex was reporting to her was no surprise. "Thank you for your help," she said.

He looked at her expectantly, probably ready to plunge right into further steps of the investigation, but for now there was nothing more to do. Not for him. Not tonight.

"Let's get some sleep," she said. With that, she climbed out of bed, and he got up as well. Briefly, something like disappointment was flitting across his face, but then he nodded and wished her a good night.

She accompanied him to the door to lock it behind him but caught herself pausing on the threshold for a moment longer. She watched him walk lightly down the hall.

No sooner had he disappeared around the corner that a floorboard creaked at the other end of the hallway—where the main stairwell was located. Penny whirled around.

At first, she couldn't make anything out, but then the silhouette of a man emerged from the darkness.

Arthur Zauner!

How long had he been standing there? Hidden in the shadows. Now he started to move and was striding down the hall—directly toward her.

"Well, did we have a romantic evening?" he sneered, his voice dripping with spite. From hard, narrowed eyes, he was gawking at her. His gaze was wandering down her nightgown.

Penny felt soiled by this examination. As if this creep wanted to undress her with his looks. She didn't dignify him with a response. Instead, she planned to just leave him standing there—or better yet, slam her door in his face.

He, however, showed amazing agility and abruptly got in her way. He put on his pinched smile, so reminiscent of a hyena.

"You women are all alike," he hissed. "To fall for a womanizer like that!"

He must have noticed her astonished look. Alex might be many things, but a womanizer?

A triumphant smile spread around his lips. "Don't tell me you didn't know? Our Diamond Prince may be a good match, but he makes eyes at *everyone*. Don't think you're special in that regard. He didn't even stop at his own fiancée's sister! And now, just after she's passed away, he's already going after the next one?"

He clicked his tongue disapprovingly, fixing Penny again with his piercing gaze. "Disgusting!" he hissed, almost spitting out the words. "Doesn't get much lousier than that, does it?"

Penny felt the urgent need to take a step back. To put as much distance as possible between herself and this man. But she resisted the impulse. Instead, she fixed Arthur Zauner in her turn with a cold stare. "I don't believe a word you say," she hissed back.

He laughed out. A harsh, rasping sound. "You think I care about that? But it's true, our Diamond Prince had something going on with both of them, at least for a while. I can prove that to you."

He leaned his shoulder against the wall, just as if he were enjoying a pleasant nightly chat with an old friend here in the hallway. "You see, I once witnessed his goings-on. Involuntarily, of course," he added quickly. "Would you like to hear the story, Miss Snoopy?"

Surely, he had been lying in wait somewhere, peering through a keyhole or listening at the door, it went through Penny's mind.

He didn't wait for her answer but began to tell his story. "It was late at night, an evening when both Mr. Adamas and I took our leave here to return to our own homes. We were standing near the coat rack, down in the hall. He put on his jacket, dug his car keys out of his pocket...and a photograph fell out. A portrait shot of a naked beauty. And I mean stark naked! Guess what: it was the little floozy. Not the older one he's engaged to. Now you're amazed, huh!"

He ran his tongue over his lips. "Our good Mr. Adamas was terribly embarrassed, I can tell you. He tried to hide the photo from me as quickly as possible, but old Arthur still has eyes like an eagle!"

He tapped his temple and put on his hyena smile. Crooked and full of teeth that were far too sharp for a human being.

21

Just two streets away from Villa Schümann was an old-established Viennese café with a beautiful garden under linden trees. The perfect place for breakfast, where you didn't have to fear finding yourself at the same table as Arthur Zauner again.

Penny was starving and ordered brioche croissants with butter and a large portion of ham and eggs. While devouring the food, she started to review everything she had learned so far in this murder case. What was important, what was not? Was Arthur Zauner just a creep or a killer, too? Had he told her the truth about Alex? Was Valerie's fiancé really in possession of nude photos depicting Niní?

She remembered the card Niní had received. Was Alex the mysterious A after all? She urgently needed a sample of his handwriting.

After breakfast, she flipped open her laptop and returned to the Heart Whisperer's website. To her delight, a chat message had come in for her. Even better, the love witch seemed to be online right now. A small green dot was glowing next to her portrait in the chat window.

The message, however, was sobering:

Sorry, dear Penelope, but I just work online. I do not offer in-person appointments.
However, I'm sure I can still help you. The vibrations I'm re-

ceive from you tell me that your heart is in great turmoil.

Phew, what a load of drivel! But the good lady wasn't entirely wrong. Penny's heart *was* in turmoil—who was she trying to fool in that regard? But knowing that much was certainly just a fluke on the part of the good witch! Surely she said something similar to each and every one of her potential clients.

Penny wondered what to answer. She began to type:

A friend recommended you to me. Niní Delight.

If there could be no face-to-face meeting, she had to get to the point online. That was against her original plan, but maybe that was the only way to get through to the heart whisperer.

The answer arrived posthaste:

Glad to hear that. What can I do for you, Penelope?

Hmm. That wasn't a helpful reaction. On the other hand, what exactly had she expected? That this supposed witch would offer to look for Niní's killer in her crystal ball? Judging from her answer, the woman didn't even know that Niní was dead. And how could she?

Penny continued typing:

Niní told me that you helped her win the heart of her dream man. Can you tell me more about how that worked out? I want the same for me.

She thought for a moment, then added a smiley face. :) Hopefully making her words look more like casual chit-chat and less like an interrogation.

If you long for the one great love, you've come to the right place. :) – the witch wrote back.

Smiley there, smiley back. But not a word about Niní. Confidentiality was probably one of the strengths of this self-styled magician. And now what?

Penny typed:

What kind of info do you need about my chosen one?

The answer was:

None at all. Your heart already knows who it wants. That's enough for the magic to unfold.

Crap. That probably meant the heart whisperer had no idea who Niní's Mr. Unknown had been either.

At that moment, Penny's cell phone rang. The number of Christy Schelling, her detective colleague, appeared on the display.

Quickly, Penny typed one last message into the chat window:

Okay. I'll get back to you! And let me know about your pric-

ing please.

She closed the laptop. That had been a dead end, then. Hopefully Christy—whom Penny had put onto Lars Simon—had better news.

"Your twenty-four-seven snooping partner, always at your service!" Christy announced as soon as Penny accepted the call. The young detective's tone sounded promising.

"Managed to find out anything?" Penny asked hopefully.

"Nothing criminal but still something interesting, I think."

"Let's hear it. Don't keep me in suspense!"

"So, our good Lars is a very busy lover. He dates a different woman pretty much every day. I've really dug deep and been able to reconstruct some of these rendezvous. I've talked to girlfriends of girlfriends of girlfriends of the women he dates. You know how that goes. Also, I did a little digging in my, uh, archives."

Christy Schelling had access to databases all but unknown to mere mortals. Penny suspected that she had a love interest or at least a good friend in high places in the police or some other agency. She didn't even ask Christy about it because this kind of information gathering was certainly not legal. But it was very useful. And in the case of a murder, the end justified the means!

"Lars Simon hasn't been in steady employment for years," Christy said. "He's not living the high life, but he's no beggar either. He has no debts. From the looks of it, he's letting the women keep him."

"A gigolo?" Penny really hadn't expected that.

"No, at least not officially. As far as I could find out, he doesn't take fixed fees. And he doesn't advertise his services either. It's more like...having a certain reputation, you know. He's known to give women a good time—on demand—and to be interested in the finer things in life. A small gift of money here, a vacation there, or with his regular girlfriends sometimes a car, an expensive watch, an art object. I suppose he sells off some of those things afterwards for his cash needs."

Watches, Penny thought, *so that's why he had approached Alex about wanting to sell some.*

"What's the best way to get to him?" she asked her colleague. "I have a few questions for this guy."

"Well, since everything with him is by word of mouth, maybe your best bet is to say that one of your girlfriends told you about him. Hopefully you can get away with that. He's certainly interested in new business, I think. Do you want his cell phone number?"

Christy had done a really thorough job.

"Yes, please," Penny said. Then she thanked her colleague, hung up, and immediately dialed the phone number she'd just noted down.

22

After Penny left the café, she directly returned to Villa Schümann. She had managed to arrange a date with Lars Simon for tonight already. Until then, she would use the time to pursue other leads. In particular one that she was very reluctant to follow. But it couldn't be helped, she had no choice in the matter.

Fortunately, no one ran into her when she arrived at the villa this time. Both the spacious garden and the house it-self lay quiet and seemingly deserted.

Penny hurried up the stairs, trying to remember where the room she was looking for was located. Alex had mentioned it only once, briefly: his *lab*, as he'd called it. A room that Valerie had made available to him for his work.

Penny had to open a few doors, but then she ended up in the right place. The lab was a small room with a large work-table. Right on top sat a futuristic-looking microscope, pre-sumably for taking a closer look at precious stones. In ad-dition, there were various lamps and all sorts of other equipment, the names and purposes of which Penny didn't know. In one corner of the room stood an old-fashioned safe that looked as if it could easily weigh half a ton. What treasures might it be protecting?

But that's not what Penny had come for. She turned to a store cabinet that took up one of the walls.

In the third drawer she pulled out, she found what she

was looking for. A notebook with handwritten entries by Alex Adamas.

Apparently, he used the booklet to record new contacts he'd made at trade shows. There were a few business cards pasted onto the pages, along with remarks that Penny couldn't make much sense of. They seemed to be measurements and prices of various gemstones.

But the content wasn't important anyway. It was all about Alex's handwriting. She turned a few pages, and her heart suddenly felt too big to fit into her chest.

The letters on the card Niní had received from the mysterious A were a little more pleasing to look at than those that filled the pages of the notebook. But that was no surprise for Penny. One took pains, after all, when writing love messages. Still, it was the same handwriting, no doubt about it.

At 7:00 p.m., Penny arrived at one of the hippest restaurants in town. Dinner at this place was part of her lure for Lars Simon.

The expenses in this case were adding up rapidly. But Lucinda wouldn't find fault with that if Penny was able to present her with her daughter's killer at the end. Hopefully.

During her phone call with Lars, she had posed as a lovesick woman in desperate need of a romantic evening.

"Would you care to have dinner with me?" she'd asked him, trying to come across as shy as possible. Then she had suggested the posh restaurant, subtly hinting that she would pick up the bill and hence was a worthwhile match.

She had also casually mentioned that her boyfriend had just dumped her but that she had booked a luxury vacation in France in two weeks' time. For two people.

"My friend—who recommended you to me—mentioned that you stood in for her ex in a similar situation," she chirped into the phone. "Maybe if the dinner goes well...?"

That was all she'd had to say. It just so happened that Lars had nothing planned for tonight. And he was looking forward to getting to know her.

When he showed up at the restaurant, he was all charming smile, attractive appearance, and best manners. A real professional. Penny let him enjoy his aperitif—then she gave up the act.

"You were friends with Niní Delight before her death," she said straightforwardly. "Was she your true love or a...client?"

Lars almost choked on his drink. His eyes snapped wide open. "You...didn't mention that Niní was the one who recommended me," he stammered.

"True. It wasn't her. In fact, no one recommended you at all. I'm a, um, consultant looking into Niní's death. A bit more closely than the police. And I've got a few questions for you."

Not exactly a subtle approach, but it wouldn't have done any more good pretending to be the lovesick single woman for a few hours first.

Lars was glaring at Penny. Gone were the charm, the smile, the attractive facade. He put down his glass and

151

wanted to get up.

Penny, however, put her hand on his. It wasn't a tender gesture but one meant to keep him from leaving.

"I think the, um, service you provide to lonely women is really great," she said, lowering her voice to a barely audible, yet insistent whisper. "And I don't want anything more than a statement from you, that's all. But if you refuse, I'm afraid I'll have to call a friend at the local tax office. I'm sure he'll be very interested in your business methods. You're no bothering with invoicing, a trade license or taxes at all, are you?"

She let go of his hand but continued to lean over the table, toward him. "Or I could ruin your reputation. With word of mouth as your main marketing tool, negative gossip could really hurt your business, I guess?"

She put on a sugary smile. "Just a few questions, I promise. And dinner's on me!"

Lars tensed his shoulders, which were really exceedingly shapely. He seemed undecided for a moment, but then with a theatrical sigh he let himself sink back into the chair. "What do you want to know?"

At that moment, a waiter approached the table to take their order. Lars went for a four-course menu of the most expensive dishes, but Penny did not object. She limited herself to a main course, followed by dessert.

As soon as the waiter had turned away again, she started to cross-examine Lars Simon. "Let's start with how you met Niní," she began.

At first he was quite monosyllabic. He emphasized several times that he'd been really fond of Niní. She had been more than just a flirt, as he put it. "Our initial date...that was a gift from a friend of Niní's. I was hired, if you will. That happens sometimes."

"Who was this friend?" asked Penny.

He declined to comment on that. "I didn't want to take the job in the first place," he said. "I was supposed to feign true feelings for Niní. I didn't want to do that. But then..."

"Then this friend promised you a generous fee?" Penny speculated.

Lars nodded, barely noticeable. "Cash in hand. That doesn't happen to me very often. I regularly receive very generous gifts, but I have to turn them into cash first."

"And this friend's name?" Penny repeated.

"She didn't want Niní to know I was hired."

"I understand that. But now Niní is dead, and we have to find out who murdered her."

"Then it wasn't...suicide?" asked Lars in a toneless voice. He seemed honestly shocked, but what did that prove? This guy had to be good at pretending. It was an important skill in his line of business.

"It was murder," Penny said curtly. "So...the name, please?"

At this point Lars probably sensed the chance to put Penny under some pressure. Or rather, to squeeze some money out of her. "This info will cost you something," he said, as casually as if he were merely commenting on the taste of his soup.

Even more expenses, Penny thought. But what else could

she do? She didn't really know anyone at the tax office, and she had no interest whatsoever in blackening Lars Simon's name. After all, she herself was operating a little, well, outside the rules.

"Five hundred euros," she offered.

"Let's say two thousand."

The guy was shameless.

"I don't even have that much on me," she said. "And I guess I can't pay by credit card?"

"Get the money. There's a bank right across the street where you can get credit card withdrawals. The ATM foyer is open around the clock. Why don't we walk over together after the main course? A few steps will do us good." He put on a smug smile.

Silent, though quite angry inside, Penny followed the guy out of the restaurant a little while later.

He stopped at some distance from the bank. "You can handle it from here," he said. He pointed to the two cameras above the bank's entrance. "I don't necessarily need to be seen together with you."

"All right," Penny replied.

Handing cash to a windy guy on a lonely street at night. That wasn't exactly what the detective manual said. But so be it.

Penny procured the necessary cash, paid Lars, then dragged him back to their table in the restaurant. He signaled to one of the waiters that the next course could now be served.

"So...the name?" Penny asked impatiently.

"She calls herself the *Heart Whisperer*," Lars said. "Some kind of love witch. I guess Niní was a client of hers. In any case, she was the woman who hired me. But it was all by email, I never met her in person. The first few times she wrote to me from a nondescript e-mail address. Probably one that could not have been traced. But one time she made a mistake. Was sloppy, I don't know. On that occasion I found the office email address of this heart whisperer as sender in my inbox. Something like that has happened to me as well, when I send messages from my cell phone. You quickly end up in the wrong mail account if you have several."

He shrugged. "Anyway. Niní must have been a special client of this heart whisperer. One to whom she gave a very bespoke service by hiring me." Again, he grinned, this time with undisguised pride in his gaze.

The heart whisperer? Penny really hadn't expected that.

"Do you have any idea why she did that?" she asked Lars. "Why she hired you for Niní? Were they friends or something?"

Lars Simon frowned. "I don't believe that. I rather thought this heart whisperer wanted to prove the effectiveness of her spells. You understand? They're all cheating! Psychics hire detectives to spy on their clients...so it's not surprising if the love witch hires me, is it?"

"What kind of time period did she book you for?"

"Actually open end. Over several weeks."

"Hmm. She must have charged Niní an exceedingly hefty fee to make such an investment in you worthwhile. I'm guessing you don't come cheap."

He twisted his lips into what was probably meant to be a grin. "Of course not! But anyway, Niní never mentioned this heart whisperer to me. I don't think she knew I was being paid. If you know what I mean. She really thought I was into her. And in the end—"

He hesitated. "That's when I really was keen on her," he added quietly, without the arrogant undertone in his voice that had been unmistakable a moment ago.

"What exactly was your assignment from the Heart Whisperer?" Penny asked.

"Simply that I should help Niní get over some other guy."

He interrupted himself, seeming to think about something.

"Funny, actually," he then said. "Niní didn't seem like she was lovesick. She was into a guy, that was all, but she was sure she could get him. There was no talk of getting over him. With me, she was just having a little fun. I'm pretty good at what I do," he added without any false modesty. "And hey, I had fun with her, too. She was hot. I liked that job!"

"So you're saying, your assignment from this heart whisperer ran...until Niní's death?"

"Well, not really." He hesitated, clasping his hands on the tabletop.

Penny gave him a scrutinizing look. For a moment she was afraid he might get the idea of asking her for more money. Impudent as the guy was, that would hardly have surprised her.

Fortunately, however, he continued with his report without any further demands. "I received the final payment from the Heart Whisperer some time ago. It must have been about two weeks before Niní's death. That's when the witch wrote me that my services were no longer needed. But I continued dating Niní. As I said, we had a lot of fun together."

"How did you get paid while you were on the job—with your client wanting to remain anonymous?"

"She sent me cash. In an envelope, by messenger. That's how we did it. I received several partial payments over the weeks."

"Hmm, I see." Penny pondered for a moment, then asked, "On the day Niní died, did the two of you have anything special planned?"

"Something special? What do you mean?"

"I don't know exactly. Something Niní was really looking forward to. She spoke to her mother the night before about how it was going to be her big day."

Lars broke out laughing. "Well, I would have been flattered! But I really don't think that was about me. We didn't even have a date for that day because her sister was having a party. To which Niní didn't invite me."

"Okay...one last thing." Penny turned and reached for her purse hanging on the back of the chair. From one of the side compartments, she fished out the card of the unknown A. She slid it across the table to Lars.

"Did you write this card?" she asked him.

He only glanced at it. "No. Definitely not. My name isn't

A, after all."

"It could be a nickname?"

He shook his head. "Nope. It's not my handwriting either."

Who are you kidding, Penny? the voice of her conscience spoke up. *You already know whose handwriting this is.*

23

That very night, Penny pulled out her laptop as soon as she returned to her operations center, as she herself had come to call the room by now.

Once again, she surfed to the website of the Heart Whisperer. Actually, she had dismissed the good lady as a dead end, but now the self-proclaimed magician had returned to the limelight. Why on earth had this woman booked a gigolo for Niní, her client? That was really strange business behavior.

Penny went to the imprint of the website, but didn't get any more information there. No civil name was given, but at least there was a postal address. An office address in an outer district of Vienna.

Penny reached for her cell. A quick glance at the display told her that it was already approaching midnight, but she couldn't take that into account now. She dialed the number of her colleague, Christy Schelling.

After the third ring, a sleepy voice answered. "Hello?"

"Sorry, Christy, it's me. I'm afraid I'm going to have to book your express screening service again. And make it super express, please!"

She was answered by a moan. Followed by: "Don't you ever take a break, Penny?"

"Yes. Of course, I do. Sometimes. But now it's urgent. No time for a break."

Another moan. But finally, Christy said, "Okay, let's hear it. Who do you want me to screen this time? Do you have a murder suspect?"

"I have a website whose owner I'd like to get to know better. Just get me everything you can find out about her, okay?" She gave Christy the web address of the heart whisperer. "How soon can you make it?"

"I'll go as fast as I can, okay? But you have to give me a few hours of sleep!"

This time it was Penny's turn to moan, albeit half-jokingly. "It's okay, Christy, I'm counting on you. And thank you!"

Penny would have liked to go to sleep now, too, but there was still something she had to do. A task that she would have preferred to postpone indefinitely.

She found Alex Adamas in his lab. The man was a night owl, she had already found out that much. Today, too, he seemed chipper, while Valerie had probably long since devoted herself to her beauty sleep.

When Penny entered the room, he was sitting at the table, bent low over one of his instruments, and didn't even seem to hear her. Full concentration. Beside him, in an unfolded tissue paper, lay half a dozen bright green gems.

"Emeralds?" asked Penny in greeting when Alex finally noticed her.

His eyes were glowing even more intensely than the gems. He seemed happy to see Penny. "Tsavorites," he explained, "not emeralds. How good to see you, Miss Sherlock! What's new?"

But when Penny remained serious, he jumped to his feet and came toward her. "Did something happen? "

Penny pulled the card with the heart balloons out of her purse and held it out to him. "This A guy—that's you," she said, "and please don't deny it again, I've had a look at your handwriting."

He came to an abrupt halt, only half a meter away from Penny. The sparkle in his eyes had gone out, which unfortunately made him only slightly less attractive. He tried to reach for the card, but Penny wouldn't let him. Not that he would end up destroying any evidence.

He frowned. "I didn't write that card," he said slowly but firmly. "I swear!"

"And what about Nini's nude photo? You didn't carry that around in your pocket either?!" She was startled at how loud her own voice sounded. She had actually wanted to remain calm and collected. But if Alex intended to lie to her face in an ice-cold way, then she had to take a harder tone. As much as she detested that.

"Arthur," he growled, his eyes darkening so that he seemed threatening all at once. "He told you about the nude photo, didn't he?"

Penny nodded. "I don't like the guy any more than you do, but are you going to deny that he's telling the truth? About that picture?"

"It fell out of my pocket, in front of his eyes. That much is true," Alex replied.

"But?"

"But it wasn't me who put it in there. What do you take me for?"

"Arthur thinks you're a ladies' man."

Alex snorted. "I so don't care what that buffer thinks I am!"

"Neither do I," Penny relented. "But still, I need an explanation. I hope you can see that."

"Let's sit down," he said flatly. He suddenly seemed very tired. Almost exhausted.

Penny took the seat he was pointing to. He gingerly slid some papers off one of the other chairs and settled down as well. Then he rubbed his temples.

"Well?" Penny asked gently, yet urgently.

"You want to hear the truth? All right. Niní took her own life. She wasn't murdered. She went to her death voluntarily—and because of me!"

"Come again?" gasped Penny. It felt like he had punched her in the face.

"You heard me. I was hoping, no, praying you would never know. Because you—oh damn, it doesn't matter now. Niní got herself into something there. She imagined that I was the love of her life and that we were meant for each other. She acted like a crazy person. She stalked me, wrote me love letters, which she slipped to me, and she tried to hit on me when Valerie wasn't around. One morning she rushed into my lab in her robe and started undressing before I had even said hello! She was just wearing some of her hand-sewn lingerie under the gown—tiny pieces, if you must know. If I hadn't taken flight, spooked like a monk's novice, she probably would have been all over me in the next moment."

"And the photo in your pocket?" asked Penny.

"I don't know. She must have put it in there for me. It was probably meant as a gift. To get me in the mood."

He looked at Penny with a pleading look in his eyes. "You have to believe me! I've done everything I can to make her understand that I love her sister. That I'm going to marry Valerie. But she didn't take it seriously."

"Did Valerie know about this?" Penny asked. "That Niní was so persistent in stalking you?"

He nodded. "Yes. I brought it up with her shortly after Niní started it. But Valerie merely dismissed it with a laugh. It's always been that way with Niní, she told me. Competition among sisters. If there was a new man in Valerie's life, Niní was after him just a few weeks later. So I shouldn't take it personally. Easier said than done!"

He was rubbing his temples, almost as if he wanted to drive away his memories with this gesture. Then he took a deep breath. "No matter what I did, Niní wouldn't give up. She kept coming up with new stunts like the robe thing. At some point I stopped telling Valerie about it. She, as I said, had no problem with it. But I did! I felt guilty, even though I really didn't do anything to stir up Niní's feelings for me! And she was dead serious. She wanted me or no one—she kept telling me that."

He paused, lowering his head. He looked at the tabletop instead of seeking Penny's gaze as he continued, "That's why Niní wanted to die, you see? Because I rejected her! I didn't murder her, and in my opinion I'm not to blame for her death. But damn it, it still feels that way!"

Penny looked at him with her mouth open. It took her a few moments to regain her speech. "And the card?" she then asked. "It's your handwriting, in spite of everything."

"Looks like it, yes. Maybe someone *wanted* Niní to believe I wrote it. It's a good forgery. But a fake nonetheless."

"And who might be responsible for that?"

Alex's attractive features hardened. "For example, someone who loves to meddle in things that are none of his business," he said with bitterness. "Someone who seems to hate every person in this house—except Lucinda. Although I can't imagine he could love anyone at all."

He didn't mention a name, but he didn't need to. *Arthur Zauner.*

"But if Niní really wanted to die because of you," Penny said, "if she did commit suicide after all, then why this poison attack on me?"

"By God, I don't know, Penny. I swear."

24

The next morning, Penny again took up position in the shady garden of the café, where she had held her working breakfast the day before. The day promised to be a glorious summer day. As if the world were a place without any problems. Without danger. Without murder.

It was only a little after ten o'clock, but Penny couldn't help herself—she dialed the number of her colleague Christy Schelling. "Do you have anything for me yet? About the heart whisperer?" she shouted into the phone as soon as Christy answered.

Her colleague groaned audibly but more jokingly than genuinely unnerved. "We're on it, Penny. Hopefully by tonight I'll have what you need. You know what my motto is: we do the impossible right away; miracles take a little longer."

Penny had to laugh—at Christy's words and at her own impatience. "It's fine. Thank you!" she said. Then she hung up.

Her good mood vanished in the very next moment when her thoughts started wandering back to Alex Adamas. She saw his handwriting in the notebook in front of her mind's eye, which so clearly resembled that on the love card to Niní. Was he Niní's murderer? Or was it Arthur, the creep with his hyena laugh?

In addition to her laptop, Penny had brought her own

notebook, which she now opened. Sometimes you just thought better on paper.

No emotions now, she admonished herself. Just the bare facts. She began to recap everything she knew about the case. Alibis, statements, circumstantial evidence, every little thing that seemed somehow relevant. The solution was hidden somewhere in this information, you just had to dig it out!

When afternoon came, Penny was still sitting at her table. She had eaten a piece of curd cake and a raspberry tartlet—and lost track of the amount of hot chocolate she had already consumed. The brain needed sugar to work—she had that excuse, after all, to work herself into a real caloric frenzy here.

At the neighboring table sat a couple in love, smooching, holding hands...which made it very difficult for her to concentrate. The thought entered her mind so spontaneously that she couldn't do anything about it: *am I going to experience something like this again?* She speared the last raspberry remaining from her tart with the cake fork. Perhaps a little too violently.

Jesus, Penny, don't be so childish. It's not the poor fruit's fault. And you still have your whole life ahead of you!

Now was really not the time for such sentimentality. And yet, for a moment, she gave herself over to a sweet daydream: what would it be like to have a man like Alex by her side? A man who was smart and attractive and funny. Who was passionate about his field, who spent his nights in the lab examining precious gems instead of zapping away the time in front of the TV. And who also shared her own passion for crime, for murder investigations.

There were only two problems. First, Alex Adamas was in love with a burlesque diva, not with her. And second, he was in the top two of her suspect list in the current murder case. Why take the easy way in love when you could opt for impossible?

A waitress showed up and asked if Penny wanted to order anything else to eat. "The kitchen will close soon, miss."

"What...yeah, sure." Penny had the menu handed to her and studied it absentmindedly. She didn't feel any real hunger.

She ordered a portion of egg gnocchi, which she gobbled down with little appetite. She hardly noticed what she was shoving into her mouth. Her thoughts were circling incessantly around the case. Next to the plate, she was scribbling in her notebook, crossing things out, adding new thoughts, but she didn't really get any smarter. She had very concrete suspicions but no real evidence. There was nothing that could be used to clearly blame Niní's murder on a specific person.

She pondered and pondered until her skull felt as if it must explode in the next moment.

Shortly after half past four—as Penny was just about to leave the café—her cell phone started to ring.

It was Christy.

Penny picked up before it could ring a second time.

"So, listen," Christy began after a curt greeting. "I brought in another colleague, and we've been working nonstop. Just for you. I drove to the address our heart whisperer put in the imprint of her website. It turned out to be some kind of office center where you can rent small units or just a mailbox. Permanently if you want, but you can also just book a conference room for a few hours. Perfect for small business owners, freelancers...and people who like to stay under the radar, if you know what I mean. Our heart whisperer definitely falls into this latter category. She only has a mailbox of sorts there, and no one knows her personally. And for the boss of the office center to hand over the data of his clients, the police would have to pay him a visit. With a warrant in their hands. He's rather serious about confidentiality."

"Crap," Penny hissed. She had hoped so much that Christy would help her make a decisive breakthrough in her investigation with some good news.

The fact that the heart whisperer shied away from the public could mean anything. Maybe just that she didn't want everyone to know who she was. Not particularly surprising in her business.

"I've also brought an, uh, unofficial contact in," Christy continued. "One who's pretty good with computers."

"A hacker, you mean?"

"What a naughty word!" retorted Christy. "But get this: he tried to find out who runs this heart whisperer's website.

Via the domain or whatever it's called. Unfortunately, no success there either. It would take a real guru, he said. The site seems to use very professional encryption technology. Something like that. Unfortunately, I know too little about it to describe it to you in detail. In any case, no luck via that route either. Our heart whisperer loves it discreet. She must really rip off gullible customers who have too much money."

Penny suspected as much, only it didn't help her one bit in her murder case.

"Is that all?" she asked Christy.

"Not quite yet. I've also put Karen, another colleague, on the case to track down a few of the reviewers who are listed on the website with their full names and their addresses. With smaller towns and fancier names, tracing these people is no problem. I don't have to tell you that. Anyway, Karen was able to contact a few of the women. Quite inconspicuously via social media. Facebook and so on. She pretended to be interested in the services of the love witch and asked a few discreet questions."

"Good idea," Penny said. "And what did she learn?"

"I'm afraid not really anything unexpected either," Christy said. "The ladies were only too happy to provide information. Without exception, they were delighted with the witch's services."

"Hmm," Penny grumbled. "How great."

"Anyway, the procedure of the good heart whisperer seems to always be the same," Christy said. "She listens— via chat—to her clients' problems or desires, then sells the appropriate incantations, potions, talismans, rituals...the whole esoteric program. I also had Karen check if any of the women had been pampered with the services of a gigolo or something similar, but there was no indication of that. No man turned up in their lives who might have been bought. None of the ladies I interviewed wanted to state exactly how much they'd paid in total for the services of the heart whisperer. I suspect a princely sum, but not that large to justify the hire of a gigolo for several weeks. Just to create the illusion that the witch's services are really effective. There's no way something like that could be profitable!"

Silence.

"Penny, are you still there? ...Penny?"

"I'm sorry, what did you just say?"

"That hiring this gigolo was certainly not worth it? Do you think that's important? If you want, I can try..."

Penny was hearing the words, but they seemed to be penetrating her ear as if through a wall of cotton candy.

A wall of cotton candy? What a comparison!

She had clearly eaten too many desserts. But who cared? A thought had just exploded in her head, no, a whole chain of thoughts. Entwined like a boa constrictor, yet compellingly logical. And that chain led to an unequivocal, if shocking, realization.

"Oh God, Christy, you're a genius!" she almost yelled into the phone. "A *potion*, that's it!" She earned a few startled looks from the adjacent tables.

"A potion?" Christy repeated. "Penny, are you all right? Maybe you should take a break after all?"

"Yes! No. Not now! I'll explain everything later, Christy. I've got to go. Thanks a million, to you and your colleagues!"

25

At Villa Schümann, preparations were underway for an early dinner. Was Valerie planning to rehearse again today? It would not come to that because tonight a very special agenda item needed to be scheduled: the unmasking of a murderer!

Penny sought out Lucinda Schümann, who was about to have dinner again away from the young people. Alone with Arthur in the dining room. "Could you please come outside and join the others?" said Penny. "I have something to tell you all."

"I don't think dining together is such a good idea," Lucinda replied with a shy sideways glance at her fiancé.

"Would you like to know who killed your daughter?" Penny blurted out.

That hit home. Mrs. Schümann got up without another word of objection and followed her. Arthur joined her, too, shaking his head, but at least without his hyena smile.

When they hurried out into the garden and headed for the arbor, Saskia and Tony were just coming up the driveway. And in the arbor itself, Alex and Valerie had already gathered. They were sitting at the table with glasses in hand. An aperitif for a balmy summer evening.

Lucinda seemed oblivious to those present. She dropped into one of the chairs and turned impatiently to Penny, "Now tell us, who is the murderer of my daughter?!"

The others, Alex in the lead, were chiming in in wild confusion: "You know? You solved the case? Who is it? Niní was actually murdered? No way!"

It took a moment for everyone to grab a chair and for the chatter to die down. Penny took a seat at the head of the table and considered how best to get started. Choosing the right words was crucial.

"I'm afraid I've followed some false leads on this case," she began, "at least one of which was deliberate."

Again, a chaotic chorus of voices erupted. "What do you mean? Who did this—"

"Let her speak," Arthur growled. "Otherwise, we'll still be sitting here tomorrow morning listening to this half-baked nonsense."

Arthur was at his most charming—but at least his words had the desired effect. The hecklers fell silent and now seemed prepared to restrain themselves a bit and be patient.

Penny nodded her head at Arthur. "Mr. Zauner was kind enough, right at the beginning, to give me the facts in this case in his, um, so inimitable way. And I started to rack my brains over a central question: how did the murderer manage to administer the arsenic to Niní? If there really was a murderer, which I very much doubted at that point. He did not stand in front of Niní and force her at gunpoint to take the poison. For how could he have left the room afterwards? The door was locked—and according to the police investigation, no one had tampered with the lock."

"Which we've all known for a long time," Arthur grumbled. "The girl emptied the poison vial of her own free will."

"That's right," Penny said.

Arthur raised his eyebrows but then grinned with satisfaction. "Then everything is settled, and we can finally—"

Penny raised her hands. "Just a moment, please, will you?"

Without waiting for an answer, she continued talking. "Niní actually drank the contents of this vial herself, of her own free will, but she didn't know it was arsenic! And she did not suspect anything after she had drunk it. Arsenic is tasteless and odorless. Nothing immediately reveals its deadly effect. If we remember, Niní spoke to her mother about her great day. *Love at last*—those were her exact words. And she laid out a beautiful dress and the hottest lingerie that she had sewn with her own hands."

Penny paused for a moment, but this time she received only expectant looks. She continued, "When Niní talked about her big day, and that she would finally find love, it could only be about the man she longed for most. She talked about him with Saskia and even with Lars Simon, who was not the one she desired. But she never mentioned a name. We only know an initial. A. It was this unknown dream man who wrote Niní a hopeful love message. On a card with heart balloons."

Penny looked around. "Now I ask you: what would Niní have drunk that helped her achieve the success she wanted with her great love? A woman like her who believed in all sorts of mumbo jumbo and even consulted a love witch?"

"I don't know. A potion?" This came from Alex. He was

probably still enjoying playing detective. But still, he also looked rather disturbed.

"That's right," Penny said. "A *love potion*—that's what Niní thought she was ingesting. At the party planned for that evening, she wanted to win her dream man over for good. With the help of a magic potion that would make her irresistible. Or bewitch him. Maybe both. I'm afraid I don't know enough about magic potions. In any case, while Valerie was putting on her sexy show that beguiled all the men, Niní would be sitting at the table with Valerie's boyfriend—and conquer him for herself! "

"Alex?" Valerie burst out laughing almost hysterically. "He's supposed to have been her dream man? You can't be serious!"

"Dead serious," Penny said. "Niní didn't know that the two of you were going to announce your engagement that night. After all, you kept it a secret. I can't say whether she would have gone ahead with her plan anyway if she had known about it. But I don't think even your engagement would have deterred her. I think she was the kind of woman who would literally walk over dead bodies for the man she wanted."

Alex did not comment on Penny's claim. But he had already admitted himself that Niní had been in love with him.

Penny continued, "What exactly Niní thought about this love potion, we can only guess. I think she had been warned, in any case, that it was a very powerful spell whose effects could be, well, let's say, quite a bit violent. That's probably why she wasn't alarmed when the first symptoms of poisoning appeared. And when she finally got really sick, it was already too late to get help. That's why she was later found apparently willing to die, lying on the bed, rather than halfway to the door to save herself."

"And how, pray tell, did the murderer slip her this potion?" interjected Arthur Zauner. "Was he wearing gloves when he handed it to her? Surely that would have seemed a bit odd, in the middle of high summer. May I remind you that only the victim's fingerprints were found on the vial."

"No one gave Niní that vial," Penny replied. "It must have come in the mail or by messenger service. The sender could have wrapped it while wearing gloves, without anyone watching them."

"By mail?" Saskia chimed in. "And Niní is supposed to have drunk that just like that? She might have been pretty superstitious, but she would never have done that."

"The package had been announced to her, of course. And it came from a woman she trusted one hundred percent—because this sender had already proved to Niní once the effectiveness of their magic."

Penny was looking into perplexed faces. "Madame Unknown, the love whisperer," she added.

"This witch is supposed to have murdered Niní?" The interjection came from Alex. He looked skeptically at Penny. "Really now...where's the motive with her? For murder? This woman didn't even know Niní very well, did she? It was just a business relationship, albeit in rather exotic territory."

"That's right," Penny replied. "Niní was merely a customer. So the love whisperer was acting most strangely. In fact, she was the one who hired Lars Simon. He's not a real gigolo, but he took a pretty penny for courting Niní. And the love whisperer was also the one who forged the love card to Niní. The one with your handwriting on it, Alex. She had to prove to Niní how effective and potent her spells were. Hence the card. After this supposed intermediate success, Niní trusted the witch blindly."

"And how is this lady supposed to have gotten hold of a sample of my handwriting?" interjected Alex. "The forgery is quite good, as you've noticed yourself."

"A really good question—which brings us a bit closer to the solution. " Penny looked around at astonished and, in some cases, rather disturbed faces. "But at first, something was confusing me," she said, addressing no one in particular. "I didn't understand how it all fit together: on the one hand, the gigolo who was supposed to make eyes at Niní in order to get her away from Alex—because that's exactly what he was hired for, in truth. And on the other hand, the card that was supposed to give Niní hope that she had a chance with Alex. The chronological order is important here, then the supposed contradiction is resolved. The gigolo came *before* the card. Because Lars' charm proved not to be strong enough, more drastic means were necessary. Murder. And the card was really only about instilling unconditional trust in the magical powers of the heart whisperer in Niní. So that she would willingly drink the deadly potion."

Penny looked over at Alex, but he had turned away and seemed to be thinking about something. He was a talented sleuth—did he already suspect what was coming now?

"So you see there is something wrong with this love whisperer," Penny picked up her thread again. "She is not a stranger who saw Niní as merely a customer. No, this self-proclaimed witch is part of Niní's inner circle of friends and family. The person hiding behind this online-only facade is among us tonight."

26

Penny's words hit the small group like a bomb. "What? You don't say! Impossible!" and other interjections came from all sides.

Penny had to make an effort to silence the hecklers and continue to make herself heard. "I have not yet succeeded—despite some efforts of a dear colleague—in revealing the true identity of this heart whisperer. They cleverly hide behind an impenetrable facade, which they probably created in the beginning just to conceal what kind of business they were in. Ripping off gullible women by means of hocus-pocus and fake magic is not a very honorable trade. That the heart whisperer would also turn into a murderer was, of course, not planned at the beginning of this career choice. But now, who's worth considering for this role?"

She let her gaze wander across the shocked faces. "How about Alex?" she asked. "He would have had a motive, in theory, to get rid of his fiancée's pushy younger sister. But that's a pretty weak reason to commit murder, isn't it?"

Alex said nothing in reply. He was just gazing at Penny with a completely expressionless look.

"How about Saskia?" she continued. "But no. Who Niní loved or didn't love couldn't have mattered to her. Besides, it was she who drew my attention to the heart whisperer in the first place. She certainly wouldn't have done that if she herself were hiding behind this facade. So, maybe Arthur Zauner is our candidate who—"

Lucinda's fiancé cut Penny off with a snide gesture. "Why don't you stop this silly game and get to the point!"

Penny was not deterred. "You may not be fond of Lucinda's daughters," she replied to Arthur, "but you didn't become a murderer because of this resentment."

Lucinda heaved a relieved sigh. "But then who?" she asked immediately afterwards.

"You won't like the answer, I'm afraid. Just ask yourself: who not only knew Alex's handwriting well enough to forge the card but also had the opportunity to deliver it to Niní here in the house? To make her believe that the message came directly from her beloved. And who had reason to be jealous of Niní for persistently pursuing Alex? Niní called him her dream man, her great love. He was the only one for her."

"Valerie?" said Alex, barely audible.

"Are you crazy?" his fiancée roared. She let out a laugh that was far too loud. "You must be out of your mind, Penny! Why would I murder my own sister?"

"Because she's been stealing men from you your whole life. Starting with Tony, for all I know, but maybe even before that."

Penny looked over at Valerie's manager, who sat paralyzed. "You put me on this track," she addressed him, "even though at first I thought, just like you, that this rivalry between sisters meant nothing. Valerie downplayed Niní's behavior as well. Even when Alex told her about how her sister was making a pass at him."

She turned to Valerie. "But in truth, Niní's behavior did bother you. A lot. I can't imagine how it must feel when your own sister always makes advances on the very men you're in love with. And successfully, if we stick to Tony's example. She simply stole him from you—and I suspect that this was not an isolated incident. Outwardly, you and Niní were close friends, perhaps for the sake of your mother and later for business. Maybe also because you didn't want to admit how much you detested her for her behavior. You wanted to be the more beautiful, the more desirable, and get rid of this hated rival once and for all. But you didn't succeed. Not even when you became a burlesque star, the epitome of feminine charisma and eroticism. You put in so much hard work, in fact, you dedicated your entire career to it—and finally, in Alex, you found the man you wanted to marry."

Penny avoided looking at Alex. She forced herself to continue speaking unperturbed: "Niní didn't even stop at your dream man. On the contrary, she convinced herself that Alex was also her man for life, the great, one true love—and then she did everything she could to win him over. She was totally ruthless and proceeded with her own single-mindedness."

"But I would never have gotten involved with Niní!" Alex protested emphatically.

Penny looked him straight in the eye. "I believe you, but Valerie knew her sister better than anyone else. She knew Niní would never give up, even after you were married. She would have continued to pursue you, and I don't know what effect that would have had on your marriage in the long run."

Alex fell silent. He looked over at Valerie, who only snorted contemptuously.

Penny continued her accusation, "Valerie must have noticed early on what was going on with Niní. That her sister had her eye on Alex. It was, after all, as I said, a familiar pattern. And that's where the little side hustle that no one knew about came in handy for her. The Heart Whisperer. How did you originally come up with this sideline?"

Valerie did not answer. On the contrary, she was now pretending that Penny didn't even exist.

"Well, then, I guess I'll have to make some assumptions," Penny said. "I imagine that while your burlesque shows may be artistically very satisfying for you, they might not make you a particularly large amount of money. Your audiences don't fill halls, and producing shows these days, even smaller ones, certainly isn't cheap? Maybe you didn't want to be in the shadow of your well-earning sister in financial matters. Or maybe you just enjoyed fooling and ripping off love-hungry women a bit? However it may be, it doesn't matter for the murder. At some point, you made a plan to get rid of Niní once and for all with the help of the Heart Whisperer."

"You're out of your mind," Valerie hissed.

"Granted, you didn't want to murder Niní right away. You first tried to get another attractive man for her—hoping that your love-starved sister would be interested in him.

Unfortunately, that didn't work out." *Lars just can't hold a candle to Alex*, Penny thought.

She did not allow herself to pursue that thought further but quickly turned to Saskia: "When I asked you who'd originally recommended the services of the Heart Whisperer to Niní, you couldn't remember very well. A friend, you believed. Or maybe Valerie."

Saskia nodded as if in a trance.

"You were probably right about the second. Valerie arranged for Niní to find out about the Heart Whisperer—and she did it so skillfully that her sister didn't suspect a thing. Then she tried to make Niní fall in love with Lars. But when this didn't work out, she saw no other choice. Niní's advances at Alex had to stop once and for all."

"But murder?" moaned Saskia.

"Love—or jealousy—is one of the oldest, and I'm afraid most popular, motives for murder," Penny said. "And the plan Valerie came up with was really clever. I have to admit that. Her chances were excellent that all the world would consider Niní's death a suicide. All she had to do was make sure that her sister trusted the love witch one hundred percent – which, thanks to the supposed interim success with Alex's card, she managed to do. The rest was easy. A magic potion, which Niní was only too willing to take. And with that, the so unbearable little sister was silenced once and for all."

Suddenly someone clapped his hands. It was Arthur Zauner. "An excellent speech, Miss Küfer," he exclaimed. "You have convinced me. After all, it was clear to me from the start that you had potential as a detective!"

Penny couldn't believe her ears.

Arthur Zauner reached for Lucinda's hand. "And what I unfortunately also knew from the beginning, my love: your daughters are no good!"

Mrs. Schümann audibly sucked in her breath. Tears were shimmering in the corners of her eyes. Nevertheless, she did not even withdraw her hand from Arthur.

Why didn't Lucinda finally send that bastard to hell?

But there was nothing Penny could do about it. Or could she?

She turned back to Valerie. "A few flaws have crept into your ingenious murder plan, I'm afraid," she resumed the thread of her accusation. "Your first mistake was to once write to Lars Simon from the Heart Whisperer's e-mail account. Your second one was the poison attack on me. That was the end of the suicide conjecture. It not only gave me proof that Niní had indeed been murdered but also that I had to look for the murderer in her closest circle."

"But the bug poison," objected Alex, who looked as if he had just woken up from a bad dream. "How would Valerie have come up with that? You must be mistaken, Penny!"

"I'm afraid not." She gave Alex a sympathetic look. "On the contrary, the bug poison came in extremely handy for Valerie. I suppose she became an involuntary witness to the conversation between Mr. Zauner and the gardener. When Robbie praised the properties of the oil beetles—but also warned of the deadly danger at the same time—it gave her an idea. After that, it was easy to research what these beetles look like. And then to collect a few specimens of them in the villa's own garden. After all, these little bugs are quite distinctive, and harvesting their poison is not difficult either. You can find all the right info on the Internet; I've checked it out myself."

Penny glanced around but didn't get any new objections. So she continued, "Mrs. Schümann told me there had been no witnesses to the conversation with the gardener, but you can never really know when you're having an argument in such a spacious garden. I'm sure Robbie's words must have been audible at quite some distance."

"Outrageous!" exclaimed Arthur Zauner. "Murder, spying—you really stop at nothing!" He bared his pointed teeth and gave Valerie a withering look.

"Two birds with one stone," Penny said. "When I was hired to investigate Niní's death, Valerie came up with another clever murder plan. She decided to get me off her neck and at the same time cast suspicion on you, Mr. Zauner. After all, you knew about the oil beetles. Valerie sensed a unique opportunity to get rid of her mother's hideous fiancé once and for all. Forgive my frankness, Mrs. Schümann!"

Lucinda said nothing in reply—and her fiancé was also speechless in the face of this insolence.

Penny continued unperturbed: "Perhaps this second motive, this bonus effect, if I may put it that way, was in the foreground of the attack on me. After all, I wasn't a serious threat to begin with. But the opportunity to get rid of the hated future stepfather by framing him for murder probably seemed too tempting."

Which I can understand all too well, she added in her mind. "Anyway, Valerie later told me about Mr. Zauner's meeting with the family lawyer, and I thought she wanted to give him an alibi for Niní's day of death. But it was only an incomplete alibi. For it was clear from Valerie's testimony that her would-be stepfather had already returned home in the afternoon and was thus a possible candidate for Niní's murder. And by telling me about the planned disinheritance, she also provided me with the proof of how much Mr. Zauner detested his potential stepdaughters – and wanted to get rid of them."

Lucinda raised her head. "What kind of disinheritance, Arthur? What is she talking about? "

Arthur Zauner actually blushed. He mumbled something that sounded like, "We'll talk about that later."

Penny fervently hoped that Lucinda would follow up on the matter and that she might finally realize what kind of person her fiancé really was.

The meeting with the lawyer could have gone unmentioned. It didn't really matter in terms of bolstering the murder charge against Valerie, but Penny just hadn't been able to resist that side blow at Arthur. Hopefully it would have an effect.

It was Alex who suddenly stood up and shot his fiancée a questioning look. "Tell me all this isn't true, darling," he demanded. His features had hardened, his voice lost all warmth.

Valerie glared at him. "Of course it's not true! It's all made up and lies. I can't believe you would believe that crazy woman?!"

"You realize that no online identity, no matter how well disguised, is truly secure?" asked Alex, unperturbed. "If you are that heart whisperer, they will find out. And by extension, the police will be able to prove the other points Penny accuses you of. You do realize that, don't you!?"

At these words, a change occurred in Valerie. Her angry look became softer, almost tender, then pleading. The next moment her eyes were swimming in tears. "I only did it because of you!" she cried and wanted to throw herself at Alex.

He, however, stretched his arms out in time and pushed her away from him. "Because of me? I never cared a whit about your sister!"

"But it was only a matter of time," howled Valerie, now completely distraught.

She wiped her eyes with the back of her hand, turning her makeup into a black-smeared mess. "Niní's always been able to conquer whoever she'd set her eyes on. *Always*, you know! And she wanted you! More than anyone else before! I just couldn't let that happen. We belong together, you and me!"

Again, she tried to nestle into Alex's arms. "Darling?" she whispered, but he backed away from her in disgust.

Whereupon she staggered, almost fell, and finally ran off sobbing hysterically. Leaving the arbor behind and heading for the house

Penny made no effort to follow her, for which she later

blamed herself. Because, as it would turn out, Valerie ran to her room, locked herself in—and drank a lethal dose of arsenic left over from her sister's murder.

27

A few days later, it was in the local papers that Valerie Delight, the famous burlesque dancer, had been unable to cope with the grief of her beloved sister's suicide and had passed away in the same tragic way.

It was Penny who had suggested this version of events to the completely shocked fiancé and the mother, half mad with pain. Why drag the whole ugly truth out into the open and cause further grief to the bereaved families when the murderer had already punished herself?

A double suicide of two attractive and successful young women was something the tabloids pounced upon like hungry beasts—that much was unavoidable but by no means comparable to a jealousy drama, including a devious murder in the family.

Penny said her goodbyes to Lucinda Schümann—and to Alex Adamas. She would miss him; she knew that already.

At the end, he gave her a hesitant hug and tried a joke to lighten the funereal mood a bit: "If you should ever be in need of a Watson again, I'll be happy to help. But please take your time. For now, I've had more than enough of murderers."

As Penny went to bed that night, tossing and turning restlessly but at the same time dead tired, the hopeless optimist in her spoke up. It was nothing more than a thought that drifted to the surface from the depths of her subconscious, just before she fell asleep. In that fleeting period between waking and dreaming, when one was no longer careful what thoughts one allows oneself.

Alex is no longer the fiancé of an irresistible burlesque diva. And he's not a murderer either. He will probably need some time to recover from this shock. But then? Who knows...

More from Penny Küfer?

THE CURSE OF THE FIRE PEARL
Penny Küfer investigates, Book 5

Penny's latest assignment feels like a walk in the park: she is supposed to ensure the safety of a world-famous ship-owner and his fiancée on the maiden voyage of a stunning new cruise ship.

But what sounded like luxury and relaxation on the high seas quickly turns into a survival trip. Instead of breathing fresh sea air and putting her feet up by the pool, Penny finds herself dealing with a deadly mystery surrounding a legendary pearl.

The first murders are not long in coming...

About the author

Alex Wagner lives with her husband and "partner in crime" near Vienna, Austria. From her writing chair she has a view of an old ruined castle, which helps her to dream up the most devious murder plots.

Alex writes murder mysteries set in the most beautiful locations in Europe and in popular holiday spots. If you love to read Agatha Christie and other authors from the Golden Age of mystery fiction, you will enjoy her stories.

Cover design: Estella Vukovic
Editor: Michaela Delaney

www.alexwagner.at

Manufactured by Amazon.ca
Bolton, ON

30333970R00113